THE
PYRAMID

Sean Carney is the author of **Where the Captain Goes,** and the playwright of **Dracula: Last Voyage of the Demeter.** His voice can be heard on the popular weekly podcasts **Scaredy Boys,** and **How Good's Footy?** He lives in Melbourne with Belinda and Charlie.

@carneyfrom55

The author would like to thank Brendan Carney, Ash Tardy, Tom Reed, and Damian Robb.

THE PYRAMID

SEAN CARNEY

1

Somewhere in the Khumbu Valley, *Winter*

Harry Bell thought he knew what he was getting into. He thought there was more time. He was wrong.

The snowfall was oppressive. It homed in on his face and settled in around his eyes. He couldn't wipe it away fast enough before it built again. His body was now as weary as his mind, burdened by the task that saw him stumbling through the darkness in the shadow of the Himalayas.

Harry closed his eyes and thought of home. His old mattress, so comfortable and worn in, it remembered the shape of his back. His stack of three pillows, which towered over his wife's singular pillow. The yak wool blanket, gifted to them by their daughter several years earlier. But those things were gone. Now so far away they may as well not exist.

He lost feeling in his fingers first: they refused the command from his brain to wipe snow from his face. Then all the feeling and pain in his feet ceased, and for a moment he was happy. The worst was over. But then reality set in. They'd numbed in the cold and now with each step he merely plodded forward without feeling, direction or hope.

He wondered if he'd strayed from the path, though the

path was virtually unseeable, and long since covered over. His headtorch battled to cut through swirling fog and snow, but he knew his best chance of survival was to keep moving.

The wind taunted him, whispering nothings and hollering intermittently. It sounded almost human, though he attributed that to his hunger, dehydration and overall weariness.

The sound brought more chill than the wind. It ran along his spine like long, iced tendrils. He looked around for any sign, but found none. By the time he looked back, it was too late. His foot was snared beneath a root and his ankle twisted painfully in its hold. He collapsed to his knees and threw out a hand to break his fall. The snow was not as cold on his face as he had imagined. Then he knew why. He was warmed — ever so briefly — by the steady flow of blood that leaked from a cut on his forehead.

Harry was dizzy. His vision blurred. His mind wandered to dark corners. How easy it would be, he thought, to never move again. To surrender to the cold. To surrender to everything. That would be warm.

Harry closed his eyes.

For the longest time, the only sound was the storm.

Then a cry.

Garbled words that Harry couldn't make sense of. But there was something in the voice he recognised. Fear. He slowly rose, covered in a thick layer of snow. He strained his ears, trying to block the howling wind.

The cry again. Louder. Carried by the night. He turned his body in its direction and plodded ahead, straining for more sounds to assure him of his course.

A new sound entered the fray. Deeper. But still faint. He

doubled his efforts and continued to inch towards whoever else was as crazy enough to be out in the storm.

Harry's headtorch flickered. He slapped his gloved hand against it and all light vanished. He stumbled in total darkness. He slapped the light again and it sputtered back on. He took a moment to regain his bearings, but not before he felt something squelch underfoot. He knelt beside it and angled the torch down. He squinted at the mass in the low light. He scooped it up in his numbed hand and held it before his face. For a moment, he couldn't breathe and when he finally did it spilled from his mouth in a gasp. In his gloved palm, he held a severed hand. Fresh blood dripped from it and dotted the ground at his feet. Still on his knees, he found the wits to move forward.

The whispers continued ahead and he continued to inch closer. As he crawled through the snow, it was increasingly stained red. His mouth hung open in disbelief as he waded through the carnage of severed limbs, and with a further jolt he recognised organs.

The whispers had grown louder and were now accompanied by the flickering of light. A small fire was ahead. Harry wiped his bloodied gloves in the snow — and fighting back the urge to gag — climbed to his feet. He limped towards the fire. The trail of dismemberment led to a figure hunched over the flames. Harry could now hear the voice. A man's voice with a detectable Irish accent. It carried over the crackling fire and the hammering storm. The words that had been ghostly whispers from afar were now clear. The man said them over and over. Slowly, and steadily.

'They do not fear, they cannot hear. They do not feel, they are not real. They cannot see, they should not be.'

Harry stopped at the sight of a glimmer. The man raised his hand in a fast movement and the firelight caught the rusted blade gripped in his hand. Something sat draped over his knee.

'They do not fear, they cannot hear. They do not feel, they are not real. They cannot see, they should not be.' The blade swung down. The thing draped over his leg stirred, and cried out. Its head tilted and in that moment Harry locked eyes with a child. A young boy, no more than ten.

'They do not fear, they cannot hear,' repeated the man with another swing of the blade. The boy screamed, and the man hurled something over his shoulder. It landed in front of Harry and he looked down upon the severed ear of the boy.

'They do not feel, they are not real,' the man repeated as he took the knife to the boy again and again, hurling pieces in every direction. Harry hadn't moved. His feet were as frozen as the terrain. He wanted to cry out for the man to stop. He wanted to rush at him and physically stop him. But the cold and fear had infected his mind and body and he stood still as a statue and watched helplessly as the man raised his knife again.

'They cannot see,' he said as he buried the knife into the boy's eye socket and popped free his eyeball. 'They should not be,' he finished as he wrenched the boy's other eyeball free. The man let the boy fall from his knee and crumple on the ground in a heap, ready to be relieved of his limbs.

The man paused his chanting, and his butchery to exhale. He wiped his blade clean in the snow at his feet. He looked above to the storm. His gaze lingered above for so long that Harry looked away from him and saw a girl. She was no more than ten, like the boy. Amidst the carnage of scattered limbs and blood-drenched snow, she was the final piece to be carved. Harry's feet were still rooted to the spot. Frozen stiff by snow, but even more so by fear.

The man reached for the girl. She struggled, but he overpowered her. She bit at his hands like an animal, but he didn't make a sound. If it hurt him, he kept the pain to himself. He pinned her down and wrenched his blade free of the snow.

Harry locked eyes with the girl. She squinted into the darkness, as the man brought the blade up towards her.

'They do not fear,' he said, as he took hold of her ear and planted the knife at the base of it. 'They cannot hear.'

'Stop!' screamed Harry, mustering what little he had left to charge at the man. His feet sloshed through the snow and the man's eyes grew wide. He dropped the girl to the ground and rose to his feet. Harry dived at the man, his hand going for the knife, but the man used Harry's momentum against him to toss him aside. He skidded across the snow and tried desperately not to pass out.

The man stood over him with the blade, a look of surprise on his face. He waited to catch his breath, and then spoke.

'They do not feel,' he said, his tone beseeching, 'they are not real.' He turned his back on Harry and marched back towards the girl.

Harry climbed to his feet. 'You can't,' he said through gritted teeth.

The man did not acknowledge him. He grabbed the girl

by her long hair. He seized her face in his hand and with his fingers he stretched open her eyelid.

'They cannot see,' he began, but Harry wrapped his arm around the man's throat and he dropped the girl once more. He elbowed Harry in the stomach, causing him to stagger backwards. The man held the knife up and pointed it at Harry. He shook his head.

'They cannot see,' he repeated. Harry ran at him. The man swung the blade and caught Harry's arm. It was deep enough to cut through his heavy clothing and draw blood. Harry grabbed at the wound, but barely had a moment to feel the burn before the man struck him on the side of the head. He fell to the ground.

Harry's vision came in and out of focus as he watched the girl crawl through the snow, climbing over blood and through limbs. Her progress was halted by a firm grip on her ankle. The man dragged her backwards and turned her onto her back. She kicked at him violently but he swatted her feeble efforts away. Again, he held open her eyelid.

Harry blinked, trying to gather his wits, as his ears rung. When his eyes opened, he watched the man's blade scoop free the girl's eyeball and hurl it into the dark. She screamed in agony as he looked down on her. There was no joy in his work. 'They cannot see,' he said as he went for her other eye. 'They cannot be.'

Harry watched the blade close in on her again. His hands clenched in the snow. He quietened the ringing in his ears and staggered to his feet. He started charging, but was already too late. He watched her remaining eye wrenched free to join the other on the ground.

Harry tackled the man again. 'Stop, you fucker, stop!'

He climbed on top of him and punched him in the face. He raised his hand again and swung down hard. But the man brought the knife up to meet it. The point buried into Harry's gloved hand and out the other side. His scream was lost in the wind. He rolled off the man and scrambled in the snow, turning it red with his blood.

'Harry,' came the cry and the both turned to see the child, on her feet and staggering towards them blindly with both hands outstretched. Her face was stained with blood and two swelling pink holes sat where her eyes once were. Harry was momentarily thrown that she knew his name but the man cared little, turning his back on her.

The girl was not giving up. She fumbled through the snow, and amongst a sea of limbs, she found a rock. She scooped it up in two hands and tripped forwards, slamming it into the man's back. He stumbled, and for the first time his face was angry. He swung the blade around wildly and connected. The steel slashed at her throat and she fell backwards in a heap. The man looked down on her body as it spasmed in the snow.

Harry took his chance, picking up the fallen rock. When the man turned back around, he smashed it into his face. The man hit the ground hard and didn't move. Harry seized the knife, before falling to his knees beside the girl.

'Oh fuck, oh fuck,' he wheezed as he sucked in air. 'What did you do, you son of a bitch, what did you do?' He placed his hands over her opened throat as blood spewed in all directions.

'Just hold on. Just hold on, okay?' He reached for his backpack and the cheap first-aid kit he'd shoved down the bottom. His shaking hands fumbled over the gauze pads as he hastily put them over her wound. It hadn't gone too deep, though the blood continued to spill. He wrapped a bandage around her throat, and then dressed the wounds where her eyes used to be.

Harry sat in the bloodied snow for several moments, his hand resting on her rising and falling chest. He looked over his shoulder at the man slumped on the ground. He reached into his bag for a length of rope, and then scurried over to the unconscious man and bound his arms and legs.

He returned to the child. Her mouth moved when he neared, but her voice was choked. The throat wound had rendered her mute for the moment.

'We need help,' said Harry as he looked around for any sign of hope. 'You need help. We have to find the Pyramid.' He heaved himself to his feet and picked the girl up as gently as he could.

'You'll die out here,' came the voice of the man. He sat up in the snow and watched them. Blood trickled down his face and into his tangled, dark beard. 'She's not long for this world. And you'll follow.'

Harry jumped at the sound of his voice. He stepped backwards. He took a breath, and steadied himself before speaking. 'Remembered how to fucking speak now, have you?' said Harry.

'I've always known how to speak.' He looked down at his bound hands and feet. He tried to wriggle free, but failed. 'You've tied me,' he said as if he couldn't figure out why.

'And I'm going to leave you here to die. You can rot in hell.'

The man shook his head. 'Soldiers don't go to hell.'

'You're not a soldier. You're a murderer.'

The man tried to stand, but failed. 'I am a soldier of God.' With his bound hands, he struggled at the zipper of his jacket. He pulled it down to reveal his neck. He wore a clergy collar.

Harry leaned forward to see better. 'You're a priest? What kind of priest kills children?'

'I've killed no children. Nor has my God.'

'You're a fucking lunatic,' spat Harry.

'And you're a fucking dead man if you don't listen to me. You'll never make it to the Pyramid. Not in this storm. Not without me.'

'I'm not going anywhere with you. I'll take my chances in the storm,' said Harry, turning to leave.

'Your chances are zero. You don't know where you are. You have a little map with a marker on it, but the snow's covered over that path. And you followed my voice down this one. You've twisted around this way and that. You're lost. I can show you how to get there.'

'How do you know where the Pyramid is?'

'Because I've lived there for the past month.'

Harry hesitated. He watched the man climb to his feet with difficulty. 'How do I know you won't kill us the first chance you get?'

'You don't. But you can leave me tied up out here and we all die, or you can cut me loose and maybe live. That sounds like better odds.'

Harry bit his lip. He gently placed the girl on the ground and looked down at her — bleeding, struggling to breath and soon to be frozen by the cold. He moved towards the priest, knife in hand. He cut his feet loose, but left his hands tied.

'Lead the way.' The man nodded and began moving. Harry bent down to pick up the girl. She was heavy, and with his backpack too he felt his knees ready to buckle, but he had no choice. He was her only hope now.

'Don't bother,' said the priest. 'She'll be dead by morning.'

Harry secured the girl in his arms and looked straight at the priest. 'If she dies, so do you.'

2

The girl survived the night.

It was morning when the Pyramid came into view. As its name suggested, the building resembled a pyramid. Amid the still-raging storm, it stood out like a beacon and dominated the landscape — no mean feat. It was surrounded by hills on all sides, and had walls of glass.. Faded national flags battled to cling to their poles against the gale.

Harry trudged forward, still holding the girl. They had fallen many times in the night, and his bones creaked like an old ship. The girl had not spoken, or barely moved. But she still breathed. Her blood loss stemmed somewhat by the bandages, but she needed more help.

The mad priest had not tried to speak with Harry again. He led them along a makeshift path. From time to time, Harry had heard the priest's voice on the wind. Always chanting. Chanting the same words, again and again. Harry had held the girl tight, waiting for the priest to turn and try finish the job, but the threat never came to pass. Now they stood at the steps of the Pyramid and Harry could breathe a sigh of relief.

They pounded on the doors, pressing in close for warmth, and listened for any sign of movement within, but none came for some time. And then the doors swung open and they each fell forward in exhaustion. The girl slid from Harry's weak grasp and slid across the floor as wind and snow poured in behind them.

Confused voices surrounded them. Gentle hands pulled them further within, and Harry heard the doors heave closed behind them. He rolled over onto his back and looked up at the triangle shaped rooftop high above. Closer to the ground he was confronted by the white lab coats of half a dozen scientists.

'Dad?' said a familiar voice.

'Evelyn,' said Harry with exhausted relief. He held out a hand for her to take, and then saw the blood and remembered that his hand had a hole in it. She looked at it, aghast.

'What happened? What the hell are you doing here?' she said.

Harry gripped her hands, and hoisted himself up. His vision was blurred and he tried to focus on her face. A face he hadn't seen in years. 'The girl, her eyes, her throat… Evelyn, the girl. She needs help.'

'It's okay,' she said as people rushed to the aid of the girl behind them. 'Dad, I need you to listen to me, okay? What happened?'

Harry took deep breaths, steadying himself. Behind Evelyn's back, the priest climbed to his feet. Harry seized Evelyn's shoulders and pushed her aside. 'Him,' he said. 'It was him, the priest. He killed them all. The children. He cut them up.'

'The priest? That… that doesn't make sense,' said Evelyn.

'He's a madman,' said Harry.

The priest turned to face them. Everyone in the room stopped moving. They all looked at him. His eyes roamed around, finding, in turn, everyone's gaze fixed on him.

One of the scientists charged forward, pushing his colleagues aside, and tackled the priest to the ground.

'You son of a bitch,' he said as he wrapped his hands

around the priest's throat. Others rushed forward to reluctantly pull him off, but not before he could land a few blows. 'You goddamn son of a bitch.'

Once they were separated, Evelyn took a small step towards the priest, as he gingerly climbed to his feet.

'Why?' she said.

The priest sniffed up the blood that trickled from his nose. He didn't look at her directly. He continued to stare around. At the people. At the high ceiling. At the row of desks, and the computers and scientific equipment that sat upon them.

'Look to yourselves. You know why.'

Evelyn glanced sideways at Harry, uncertainty on her face. 'What the hell are you talking about?'

The priest turned his full attention to her now. 'The shepherd does not yield to the flock.' He didn't break eye contact with her. He didn't even blink. Harry's tired muscles tensed, bracing for the fight. But no fight came. The priest fell to his knees and held out his hands to be tied. A man rushed forward moments later and bound the priest's hands tight.

'What are you going to do with him?' said Harry. Evelyn ran a hand through her hair, and he noticed that she looked much older than the last time he'd seen her. He reminded himself that it had been a long time.

'We have somewhere we can hold him. But outside of that, we can't do much until this storm clears. We can't call it in to anyone, the damn…'

'Radio's fried?' said Harry, cutting her off.

'Yeah, that's right,' she said, and then she understood.

'But of course, you know that, otherwise you wouldn't be here.'

'I tried everything. I couldn't get through. I didn't find much help in the matter either,' said Harry.

'People are happy to forget that we're out here, in the middle of nowhere.'

'How long have you been cut off for?'

'About six weeks. The storm won't kick. Winters are hard here.'

Harry steadied himself. He gently took her arm and led her away from the other scientists. 'Evelyn, I had to come.'

'What's happened?'

'Your mother… She's dead.'

Behind them, some of her colleagues looked up at her sadly. For the longest time, Evelyn said nothing at all. When she finally did, her voice was soft. 'How?'

Harry shook his head. 'They're still figuring it out. One minute she was fine, and then… She wasn't. I'm sorry. I've come to bring you home, for the funeral.'

Evelyn reached for Harry's hand. She rolled it over in hers until she felt the bandage, and saw the blood. 'Dad, we have to have this looked at.'

'Evelyn, I…' he began.

'Dad, we need to get you better first.'

Evelyn's grip slipped at the sound of a scream from below. There were several moments of silence in which everyone looked from each other to the floor at their feet. Then the scream again. The sound of it moved in a spiral, as if climbing stairs, circling them until it burst through the heavy metal doors at the end of the room. Two doctors carried a stretcher. A man writhed in agony on it, his screams bouncing off the walls. Evelyn and the others rushed towards him. Harry stood at the rear, craning his neck for a glimpse through the white jackets of the others. The man's shirt was slashed, and Harry caught glimpses of deep cuts in his chest. Hands tried to stem the bleeding, but nothing could stem his screaming.

'Get him to the infirmary,' said Evelyn.

'They've got their hands full with the girl,' said one of the women carrying the stretcher.

'Just do it, there isn't time,' said Evelyn. The stretcher was carried away and down a hallway. She turned back to Harry and looked at his bloodied hand. 'You might have to wait to get that looked at.'

'That's fine,' he said and nodded to her.

She looked at him for a moment, in all the chaos, and smiled. 'It is nice to see you, Dad, despite all… all of this.' She turned to follow the others to the infirmary, but Harry called out, stopping her.

'She knew my name,' he said to Evelyn's confused face. 'The girl… out there, she called me Harry. How did she know that?'

'The photo on my desk,' said Evelyn with a small smile. 'I have a photo on my desk, of you and… Mum,' her voice trailed off.

After a moment, it returned. 'She once asked about you.'

3

Several hours passed while the team frantically worked on the injured man and child. Harry filled the time trying to forget about the pain in his hand. He wandered around, though could only go so far. Heavy metal doors blocked his path at the end of the room, and he noticed a key card was required to enter. He looked at the computers and research equipment, though in truth most of it was beyond his comprehension. Climate charts and statistics were strewn everywhere he looked. The walls of the Pyramid themselves were glass and completely see through. That might have been nice on a clear, sunny day, but right now all Harry could see was a vacuum of oppressive whites and greys.

Harry sat down and stared at the windows like they were a television. His eyes drooped, edging closer to exhausted rest. But he found no respite when he closed his eyes. All he saw was bloodied snow and carnage.

Harry's eyes snapped open, and he was roused by a medic. 'I'm Dr Ming,' she said with a smile and held out her hand for him to shake. Harry shook it with his good hand, while the pain in the other came back like the tide.

Dr Ming's smile was replaced in his head by the image of a bleeding, eyeless face. It took him a moment to shake the thought away. 'Where's my daughter?' he said.

'Dr Bell will be along soon. There's a lot happening, as you can imagine.'

'And the girl?'

'She's a fighter. But… it won't be easy for her,' said Ming as she led him to the heavy metal door and scanned her card. The doors opened and he followed her down a long hallway. He glanced at the closed doors as they passed. He wondered which locked door held the priest.

'You don't have to worry about the priest,' she said, as if reading his mind, 'he's not going anywhere. At least, not until the storm passes.' She walked into a room and motioned for Harry to take a seat, and then began unwrapping his bandage.

'Who were those children?' said Harry.

Ming took a moment, finishing removing his bandage, then she looked up at him. 'Relatives of people who work here, I'm afraid.'

'Were any yours?'

'No,' said Ming, smiling a little with relief.

'And the child? Does she have family?'

'She has people here, yes.'

Harry nodded. 'Good. That's good. Hell of a place to be alone.'

Ming took a fresh bandage from a drawer and tore the plastic. 'Can I call you Harry?'

Harry nodded.

'Harry, I'm afraid to say your fighting days are probably over. Unless you like using one hand.'

Harry smiled. 'I think I'll get by. Not much fighting in my line of work.'

'What do you do? Dr Bell doesn't really talk about home.'

Harry took a moment as that news sunk in. He wondered when his daughter had become so closed off. Perhaps she was embarrassed of him. 'I'm a teacher,' he said finally.

Ming wrapped the bandage around his hand and pulled

it tight. 'Tell me if it's too tight, okay? What are you, like, a science lecturer or something?'

Harry chuckled. 'No, no. High school history teacher. Nothing glamorous.'

Ming stuck a small pin through the end of the bandage. 'History is important.'

'Try telling that to a bunch of fifteen-year-olds,' he said as he flexed his hand.

'Too tight?'

'No, it's fine. Thank you.'

Ming began packing her equipment back into a drawer. 'You know, you might be the craziest high school history teacher I've ever met. Stumbling through a storm, in the Khumbu of all places.'

'Yeah, well, you guys ought to fix your phones.'

Ming smiled. She handed Harry a bottle of pills. 'Take these for the pain. You might not feel it now, but you will in the night.' She stood up and walked to the door. She lingered in it for a moment, before turning back. 'What did your history books tell you about this place?'

'The Pyramid?' he asked, and she nodded. 'Not much at all. About as much as Evelyn told us when she came up here. Leading high-altitude research facility. Cold. Isolated. I know there's a landing strip outside, if a chopper can get a clear run'.

'That your plan to get home?'

'If I can. It'd be a hell of a lot easier than going back the way I came,' he said with a smile.

'Anything else?' she asked.

'Why do I feel like your quizzing me?'

She smiled. 'You've come a long way for a place you don't know much about.'

'I'm here for my daughter.'

'This place doesn't make you curious?' she asked, leaning in.

'I don't care about weather reports.'

'I'm not talking about weather reports.'

'Then what the hell are you talking about?' He became aware that his voice had lowered to match hers, both of them now whispering.

'I haven't been here long. But I can tell you this, they don't like visitors. Because visitors ask questions.'

Harry leaned in, closer still. 'I didn't have any, until you put them in my head. What are you playing at?'

Ming put her hand atop his bandaged one. 'You need to be careful here. You must be. The priest… he wasn't careful.'

She looked at him for a long moment before slowly backing from the room.

'Rest. Take all the time you need,' she said with a pleasant smile, her voice returning to normal volume. She closed the door, and Harry sat on the bed wondering what in the hell she was talking about.

4

Harry's hands clawed at the snow. It was white on his dark gloves. He held a fistful of it and let it trickle out like sand. The snow turned red and blood poured from his hands onto the ground. An eyeball rolled from his palm, falling to the ground, where the impact bruised it like a grape. The pupil turned as if to face him. It glimmered yet there was no light. It was night, and all was dark.

Harry woke with a jolt. He glanced at his watch and groaned as he saw that he'd been asleep less than thirty minutes. The pain had woken him. Ming was right. He popped the lid off the bottle and swallowed two pills. He looked around for water but saw none.

Harry left his room and poked his head out into the corridor. It was empty. He slowly crept out, unsure why he was being so cautious. Ming's rambling words rattled in his head. But he knew everything would be fine once he could sit down with his daughter. Once they could plan their return home. But his first task was to find a glass of water.

He walked the halls of what he figured to be the infirmary section of the facility. It suddenly struck him that he didn't know how big this place was. All he'd really had to go off was an online search, but even that was limited. It showed images of a pyramid shaped building and little else. No mention of the interior or its size.

A sound stole his attention. He moved towards it. Another locked door greeted him at the end of the hall. He stared at it, but only for a moment as a murmur caught his ear. To his left was a door, slightly ajar. He pushed it wider and took a small step inside. Stirring in a bed was the wounded man who was on the stretcher earlier.

'Who's there?' he slurred. 'Show yourself.'

'Sorry,' said Harry, entering cautiously. 'I don't mean any trouble, I just heard you from down the hall.'

'I need a cigarette, you got one?' he asked.

'No, I don't smoke.'

'Why are you here?' the man asked, his expression pained by the effort of speaking.

Harry held up his bandaged hand. 'Getting fixed up. My name's Harry.'

The man shook his head. The shaking ran through his whole body. Harry put a hand on him, to try and keep him still but the man slapped it away. 'I mean, why did you come here?'

Harry leaned back a little, surprised by the hostility in the man's tone. 'I'm here to see my daughter.'

The man continued to shake, and cough. His breath wheezed out in cold puffs of cloud. 'You go back where you came from. There's nothing for you here. Nothing you want to see.'

Harry put a hand on his shoulder, a little annoyed now. 'What does that mean? What's everyone implying about this place.'

'Not implying… imploring. Leave. Nothing lives here.'

'I told you,' said Harry, his voice rising, 'I'm here for my daughter.'

The man babbled a string of words that made no sense to Harry's ears. He wondered if they were in another language. The man said the words again, but softer. Harry was concerned.

'Have they given you something for the pain?' The man didn't answer. Harry stood up and made for the door. 'I'll go find Dr Ming.'

'Do you still dream?' the man asked, his question stopping Harry from leaving.

'What?' asked Harry, turning to face him.

'Since you've been here, have you dreamed?'

Harry racked his brains at the odd question. 'I… I don't know. I've barely had a moment to sleep. Not that I really want to'

The man nodded. His shaking had stopped. His voice was still pained, the slashes on his chest still rose and fell with his ragged breathing, but he still talked. 'It's harder here. To sleep… to dream. They don't say that when you start, but everyone learns it fast.'

'I'll see if I can find the doctor.'

'I remember growing up,' he continued, as if he hadn't heard Harry. 'In Africa. None of this altitude. None of this snow, or cold. Village I grew up in, all the ladies were making stuff. Every day making something new. Knitting and sewing and wicking. My mama always made these things that hang in your room. Some parts they call them dreamcatchers. You know them? You know what they do?'

Harry nodded, but the man went on to explain anyway, and Harry wondered if he even knew he was there anymore. Was he talking to him, or just himself?

'My mama made them, and she always said you had to hang these in your room and they'll ward off the spirits that come for you in your dreams. She swore by that. For years, she made them, and for years we all listened, and we all used them, and we all kept warding off them spirits. And when I went off to study, she made me one. And when I got my first job, my first real job, she made me one. Everything I did, she made one. I got this job here, she made me the biggest one she ever made. Told me it was special. Said I had to take it, because away from home, in the middle of nowhere, in the snow and cold and isolation… well, that's when I needed it the most. So, when I got here, I put it up in my room and some of my colleagues wondered if I was a bit crazy, but I kept it up because I knew it'd make my mama happy. Truth is, it made me happy too. I can't remember a time in my life when I didn't sleep under one of them. But then sleeping gets hard. Sometimes days on end without respite. And you figure that's normal. That's your body adjusting to the new surrounds. Then you don't remember your dreams. Maybe you don't have any. You're lucky if you close your eyes for five minutes on end and they stay closed. It's a weird thing, man. To not have dreams… I guess, I guess there was once this safety in dreams. Of knowing that that's the only place you see monsters.'

Harry stood in the doorway watching the man trail off. 'What do you mean?'

'That a monster doesn't care if you pinch your arm. Because the dream doesn't end when your eyes are open,' he said, trailing off in little more than a whisper. Harry stepped in to hear him, but he stopped talking, his eyes rolling over. The rattle of his breath returned. He turned to Harry, as if seeing him for the first time. 'I need a cigarette. You got one?' he asked.

Harry looked at him for a long moment. 'No,' he said. 'No, I don't smoke.' He stepped backwards towards the door. 'I'll find the doctor.'

5

Harry sat at his daughter's desk. It was stacked with files. In fact, the chair had also been loaded and he had to move everything off of it just to get a seat. He sat, and he waited. He flicked through some of her work absent-mindedly. He was never too sure how to talk about her work. Altitude research was a far cry from the French revolution of his classroom lessons.

'You going to grade my papers?' The voice startled him. He turned to see Evelyn standing behind him.

'I wouldn't know where to start.'

'The first sentence?' she said, as she dragged another chair around to sit beside him. She reached out gently for his hand. 'How is it?'

'It'll live,' he said.

'Sorry for all the chaos. This is normally a very boring place. The commotion has people a little…'

'Rattled?' he offered. 'I've had some strange conversations. People here are on edge.'

'The winters are…' she began.

'The winters are tough,' he s-aid, interrupting her.

'Are you angry at me?'

'I'm not angry. I just… I told you your mother was dead, and then I haven't seen you for hours.'

'There's a bit going on here, in case you missed it?' She rolled back a little in her chair and stared out the giant window beside her, where dark fog swirled. After a long time of staring into the storm, she turned back and faced him. 'Tell me how it happened.'

'They don't know.'

'Was there any warning?'

'No, it just happened.'

Evelyn hesitated. 'You… You were with her, at the end?'

He nodded.

'What was it like, to see?'

'What do you mean?'

'Did she feel it? Did she feel pain?' she said, leaning in towards him.

He reached out his hand and took hers. He held it softly. 'No, no pain. None that I could tell. She just reached out and took my hand like I have yours now, and she looked at me, and she smiled. Do you remember her smile? Like the one you see in the mirror. You two always had that.'

'And then what? Did she do anything? Say anything?'

'She said just one thing. She said your name. Then she slipped off beyond, that smile on her face. You on her mind. Take comfort in that, Eve. That she didn't hurt. There was a peace to it.'

She squeezed his hand. 'I'm sorry you had to be there for that.' He squeezed hers back.

'Tried calling. Tried the embassy. Tried everything. Knew I had to come get you.'

Evelyn stood up and shuffled some papers on her desk. She cleared her throat. 'The girl looks like she's going to make it.'

'That's good,' said Harry, annoyed at her change of subject but relieved for the girl.

'But she's blind. Can't speak either, least not for the moment. His knife saw to that. She's lucky she didn't bleed out. Has you to thank for that. Brave thing you did. Stupid to be out there, but you saved her life.'

'What are you going to do with him — the priest?' asked Harry.

'Try to stop people here from killing him.'

'Would they be wrong to?'

She held his gaze for a moment, then looked to the ground. 'No. Probably not. But we're not like him. What he did was despicable. Unforgiveable. But the storm ties our hands.'

'You can't radio out either?'

'No. We'll have to hold him until the storm passes, and then send for help.'

'How are you going to hold him?'

'In a locked room.'

'This is a research base, not a prison.'

'He's bound to a table, behind a locked door. He's not going far.'

Harry heaved himself from the chair and walked towards her. 'Why? Why did he do it?'

Evelyn looked away from him. 'I don't know. He won't say. Or can't.'

'Has he said anything?'

'Just the one thing,' she said, and Harry nodded, understanding her. 'Over and over.'

Harry slumped back into his chair. He ran a hand through his dirty hair. He remembered that he hadn't showered in days. 'He told me he was living here, before.'

She nodded. 'That's right. For about a month. Priests come and go.'

'Why do you have a priest here?'

She smiled. 'People like feeling like God is around.'

'You don't agree?'

'You saw the flags out front? Scientists and research operations from all over the world. My god, his god, her god. One priest doesn't exactly cater to all needs. They're pebbles on the beach. A waste of resources.'

Harry looked at her squarely. He was surprised by some of the words that came from her mouth. He couldn't judge her though. She'd grown older, and worldlier than he ever could sitting in a classroom. 'Faith can help people through hard times.'

'Is it helping you now?'

He measured his response. 'I'm probably not in the frame of mind to answer that. But I have to believe in something.'

'I believe in science,' she said.

Harry walked to the window and put his hand against it. He was surprised it didn't feel cold, but figured it was about as thick as glass could be.

'What does your science say about the weather? When can we get out of here?'

'It's not that simple,' she said.

'Haven't made any solid plans yet. But we can't leave it too much longer,' he said, not hearing her.

'I can't just up and leave here.'

'If we can get a break in that storm, we've got to try and get that helicopter up I guess.'

'We're at a very important stage in our research.'

'Is there someone here who can fly it?'

'You're not listening to me.'

Harry finally heard her. 'Wait, what?'

'I can't leave. We've made an enormous breakthrough. We've been building towards an outcome for years.'

'She's dead,' he said.

'I just can't.'

'Your mother is dead. She needs to be buried. We need to bury her.'

'Dad…'

'I can't believe we're even having this conversation.'

'Dad, my work is important.'

'Is your mother not important?'

'That's not fair.'

'Dropping dead isn't fair. Waiting in a cold morgue for your daughter to take time off work isn't fair. Nothing is fair. We're going home.'

'I'm not a child anymore. I don't have to do what you say, and I have responsibilities here that I can't ignore. It's that simple. I'm terribly sorry that mum has died, but I can't leave. You don't understand. We've had an enormous breakthrough, and to leave now would be to throw my team to the wolves.'

'Instead you'll throw your family to the wolves?'

She stood up and walked towards the window. 'Dad… it's not a this versus that thing. Of course I want to be there for her, and for you. I'm halfway around the world…'

'I know, because that's how far I came.'

'I didn't ask you to do that.'

'You didn't have to. We're family. That comes first. Not work.'

Evelyn folded her arms. 'I'm staying. And get comfortable too. You were crazy to try and come through that storm, and it's a miracle you survived. But I won't let you go back out into it, do you hear me? You're not leaving until that storm does.'

'When it does clear, we're going home. Together.'

'I guess we're waiting for the storm then,' she said, as she began to walk away. 'Try and get some rest.'

'They tell me sleep isn't easy here.'

'Who?' she said, turning back.

'Everyone.'

She smiled. 'We're a superstitious lot.'

'I'll keep an eye open for monsters in the night,' he said with a smile.

'There are no monsters out here. Only stories.'

'Tell that to your man in the infirmary.'

She hesitated for a moment. 'He's not himself. Altitude madness has him in a grip. Mad men see what they want to see.' She walked away, reaching the metal door and swiping her key card.

'Why do you think he came back here — the priest?' said Harry.

'I don't know,' she said, turning one last time.

'He could have killed me and run away. But he came back here. He knew he'd be locked up, or even killed. Why… Why the hell would he do that?'

'Perhaps he thinks his job's not finished.'

'God's job, he would say.'

'Faith is just a small thing in the wind here.' She looked at him for a long moment, before swinging around and walking down the corridor. The door closed behind her. Harry stared out the window as a crow was caught in a gale of wind and spun like laundry before slamming into the thick glass. Within moments, it's blood was crusted with swirling ice and dirt.

6

The child's chest rose and fell steadily. Harry sat silently in a chair beside her bed. The silence of her room was only punctuated by her rattled breathing and the occasional beep of the equipment that monitored her. The walls were thick enough that he couldn't hear the gale outside. He looked around the room. Everything was stainless steel and it made him shiver.

Every so often, the girl would make a sound. But it was never more than a murmur. Harry looked at the fresh stiches that held her throat together. He looked at the thick bandages wrapped around her face and covering where her eyes once were. A small amount of blood had formed around the edges, like her soul building at the boundaries of her eyes and trying to break free. Harry wondered when, if ever, they might stop bleeding.

He began drifting into the half-way world that he had floated to since arriving. Somewhere between awake and asleep. An uncomfortable place where his weariness didn't dissipate, and his eyes grew ever more tired. A place where he saw horrors that he tried desperately to forget, but knew he never would. He was roused this time, not by a voice or words but by her touch. The girl reached out and took his hand. His eyes snapped open and he looked down at her dirty fingernails. Underneath them was filth and blood and perhaps even the flaked skin of the priest who had maimed her.

'Hey there,' he said, as he closed his other hand over

hers. 'You gave me a scare. But it's alright. He's not going to hurt you. Nobody's going to hurt you.'

Her head moved left, then right, looking around the room, but not seeing. She took her hand from his and reached out, feeling the fabric of the bedsheet. Her breathing quickened. Her mouth tightened. Harry could smell the panic. He reached out for her hand.

'You're in the infirmary. In a bed. Those are the sheets you feel.' Harry looked around for more things to describe. 'The bed frame is steel. Everything's steel. It's bright in here, too bright. But it's safe. You don't have to be afraid. That man is gone.'

The girl shook her head.

'Yes. He's not a problem for you anymore. You're safe.'

She shook her head more. She opened her mouth, trying to speak, but the only sound was strangled air escaping. She put her hands to her throat and rubbed the pain. She felt the stitches, and the panic grew. Her breathing grew heavier, and heavier. She tried to sit up, tried to get out of bed, but Harry pushed her down with a gentle, yet firm hand.

'You have to rest. First, you have to breathe. I'll get Dr Ming,' he said as he stood up. But before he could make for the door, her hand seized his with a grip much tighter than he would have thought. She yanked him back in.

Her cracked lips moved, trying to form words. Harry thought she must need water and reached for a glass, but she slapped it away. It shattered on the ground. Harry looked over his shoulder, hoping that the noise might draw some assistance. The girl's lips continued to move, she held her throat, as if worried the stitches might pop at any second. Sound came from her mouth. The same sound, over and over. Finally, Harry registered it as a 'P', but had little idea what that meant. She let go of his hand and waved her own through the air. Harry looked at it in bewilderment. But then she steadied herself and her hand movements became more controlled, and he finally realised what she meant.

'Pen!' he said, as if he'd cracked the atom. 'You want a pen?' She nodded, and her breathing slowed a little. Harry reached into his pocket and handed her a pen. He stood and rummaged in his pockets for a scrap of paper. He found his airline ticket. He handed it to her and helped her put the point of the pen on it.

Harry heard footsteps down the end of the corridor. 'In here,' he called, and heard their pace quicken. The girl continued to scribble on the page. Harry heard two sets of footsteps, nearing the door. The girl finished writing and thrust the note into Harry's hand. He opened the creases and stared down at the note. It was just a single word. Harry stared at it for a moment. Then he looked at the girl, and she looked back at him. Even without eyes, he could almost feel her see him.

Evelyn and Ming burst through the door, out of breath. Harry stuffed the note into his pocket before they could see. Evelyn looked at them both.

'What's going on? We heard a noise.'

'She broke a glass,' said Harry, stepping forward. 'I was just sitting here and she woke, and then she had a little… I guess, panic attack, you would call it.'

Dr Ming stepped forward and checked on the girl. 'She seems okay now,' she said to Evelyn.

Evelyn looked Harry up and down. 'What were you doing in here?'

'Just seeing how she was doing,' he said. 'Is that a problem?'

'No,' she said after a moment. 'No, not at all.' She looked down at the bedside table, and the pen. 'How did she get that?'

Harry turned to look at it, he reached out and took it. 'Oh, that's mine. I was going to do some writing, but realised I didn't have any paper.'

'Don't bring it in here again. She can't have a pen.'

'How's she supposed to communicate, without writing it down?' he said.

Evelyn pulled him aside, away from earshot of the girl. She lowered her voice. 'We're still monitoring her. I don't want any sharp objects near her, not with what she's been through. There will be time for communicating, but first we need to get her stable, okay?'

Harry looked at the girl, as Ming gently held her hand and spoke to her. 'Yeah, sure, no problem.'

The pair moved back towards the bed. Evelyn cleared her throat. 'Dr Ming and I need to run some tests now, Dad, if you wouldn't mind.' She held out a hand toward the door. Harry looked from his daughter to Ming, and then to the child. He gave her a little reassuring smile as he left the room, but remembered that she couldn't see it. Evelyn closed the door behind him.

Harry walked down the hallway. He glanced over his shoulder as he neared the corner. He was alone. The hallway was darker. The lights thinned out. Though one still shone bright at the end of the hall. It lit the heavy metal door he had yet to see behind. He stared at it for a long moment, before moving away.

He worked his way through the facility. It was late. Most people were sleeping, or trying to. He entered the main control hub, walking past rows of computers. He finally stopped at Evelyn's desk. He wheeled out her chair, and it squeaked in the otherwise unoccupied room. He took a seat. Her desk was tidier than it had been. He could see it clearly. Her stationary, her work, her calendar. He could see it all clearly.

The only thing he couldn't see, was the photograph of he and his wife. He bit his lip. It bothered him. But not nearly as much as the note stuffed in his pocket. He looked around again, making sure he was alone. He pulled the scrunched airline ticket out and held it before his eyes. He looked down at the single word scrawled roughly upon it — 'Catherine' — and he wondered why the child he barely knew had written the name of his dead wife.

7

Harry stood outside as the elusive sun crept from behind a cloud and warmed his face. The warmth lasted barely a minute, swallowed by swirling clouds, but the wind was steady. The sky hadn't been so clear in days, maybe even weeks.

Harry sloshed through the snow and made his way to the helipad. A helicopter lay waiting, frosted over in the cold. The man the scientists called Wild Bill attacked the ground with a shovel. He was about thirty, with a solid mountain-build. He buried his shovel into the ground around the helicopter and cleared away ice and snow. Harry finally reached him. 'You the guy they call Wild Bill?' he asked.

Wild Bill stopped shovelling and squinted up at Harry. The light bounced off the white snow in all directions, and even in winter, sunglasses were handy. 'Sounds a bit silly coming from a stranger, but yeah that's what they call me. You can just call me Bill.'

'Alright, Bill. I'm Harry,' he said as he held out a hand. Bill removed his glove, and Harry did the same, not wanting to be rude. He regretted it immediately, for the bitter cold sniffed out his exposed skin in an instant and began its attack.

'Why do they call you Wild Bill?' he said as he stuffed his pink fingers back into his glove.

'Because I fly in the wild storms,' Bill replied, putting on his own glove. He smiled at Harry. 'Not too imaginative from a bunch of scientists.' Both men laughed.

'Your daughter, she's the big boss, huh?'

Harry picked up a spare shovel and started helping clear the ice. 'I don't know much about it, to be honest. She used to write to her mum and I more when she first started. But that was a long time ago. How long has she been in charge?'

Bill stopped shoveling and scratched his thick beard. 'I'd say about six weeks or so,' he said finally, before continuing to shovel.

'That's about the time when we stopped hearing from Eve so much,' said Harry. 'I guess the workload kind of took over.'

'Probably. I don't pretend to understand half of what the lab coats say, to tell you the truth. I just fly people and things in and out.'

Harry's shovel clunked into the concrete at the base of the helipad. He was glad to be doing something active. He felt like he'd sat around, waiting and doing nothing since he arrived.

'She used to write to us, and sometimes email or call. But less so as time went by. And then communication with this place has become so damn frustrating these last few months. And now nothing works at all... This place is a bit of a mystery.'

'Only if you care about the mystery.'

'You don't?' said Harry, surprised.

Bill shook his head. 'Only way to get your job done properly. I worry about flying. I let the scientists worry about their science shit.' Bill's shovel clunked into the concrete too. 'Thanks for the help. Should get this big rig up this afternoon, if the weather holds.' He gave the helicopter a gentle tap with the end of the shovel.

'Got any room for a couple of passengers?'

'I can take a couple. Good time to go, I've seen weather turn bad fast, and who knows when you'll get another chance.'

'Alright, good. I'll get my stuff together,' said Harry, as he turned to leave.

'Who's the other passenger?' shouted Bill, pulling Harry back.

'My daughter.'

Bill smirked. 'Good luck with that.'

Harry ignored him. But a thought occurred to him. 'When are you taking the girl down?'

Bill looked confused. 'What girl?'

'The one who was attacked. Surely she needs more extensive medical care?'

'No plans there, as far as I've been told. They think they can take care of her here,' said Bill.

'And what about the priest? Are you taking him down?'

Bill laughed. 'You ask a lot of questions, Harry. You obviously haven't been here long,' he said, and then said nothing for a time. Harry continued to look at him until he felt he had to answer. 'I'm not taking the priest down, no.'

'He's staying here?'

'There's people coming for him,' said Bill.

'Which people?'

Bill took a moment to answer. He chewed his lip, as though weighing what, and how much to say. 'Soldiers. Soldiers are coming.' Nothing being said made much sense to Harry. He scratched his head, and pondered it all. He opened his mouth to speak again, but sensing another question, Bill cut him off. 'Look man, I don't have answers for half the shit you're wondering. Now, if you want to get up in the air and out of here, then give me some space so I can get this rig ready, okay?'

Harry nodded. 'Yeah of course. I'm sorry.' Bill nodded with a small smile to say it was fine. Harry turned to slosh his way back through the snow, but one more nagging thought turned him back.

'I just have to ask…' he began, as Bill sighed and looked up from his work to meet Harry's eyes. 'The man who was in charge, before my daughter,' he said.

'Dr Martin,' said Bill.

'Yeah, Dr Martin… How did he die?'

Bill turned back to the helicopter and wrenched open the door. He climbed into the cockpit. 'Go ask your daughter,' he said as he began testing the engine, and the blades slowly spun and cut through the light snowfall that resumed around them.

Harry looked away from Bill and the helicopter, and looked to the Pyramid. In the high window, looking down on him, was his daughter. He held her gaze for a moment, before offering a wave. She looked down at him and, after a long moment, returned it.

8

'We need to take this chance while the weather is on our side,' said Harry, keeping his voice low so as not to draw attention.

Evelyn sat at her desk, while her colleagues fluttered around the workplace. It was all hands on deck. She didn't look up from the report she was scribbling notes on.

'Bill said he's taking off in the afternoon.'

'Wild Bill,' said Evelyn with a grin.

'I'm serious, Eve. We can get out, at least as far as Namche, and then hike down to Lukla if we must.'

She turned to face him, the grin gone from her face. 'Keep your voice down,' she hissed, glancing at her colleagues. 'We've had this discussion already. I'm in charge here. These people look to me to lead. To make decisions. How can I do that from halfway around the world?'

'Why are you in charge?' said Harry.

'Because I was chosen.'

'And before you, Dr Martin, how did he die?'

'How did you…? Wild Bill told you.'

'How did he die?'

She put her pen down and closed her report. 'He killed himself.'

'Why?'

'He didn't leave a note. It caught us all off guard. But we were able to keep working.'

'There you go again. A man died, and all you can think of is work.'

She stood up to face her father. She was a foot shorter

than him. 'Look where you are. Look around at this place, at these people. We're not the same as what you see back home. We don't drink ourselves stupid. We don't go out dancing on the weekends. We do our work. We are our work. It's as simple as that. You might think it cold that we didn't fall apart and mourn Dr Martin, but what we do is honour him by continuing the work. That's all we can do. The work continues.'

'And this work, this important work that keeps you away from your family… you can't talk about that?'

'What do you want to know, Dad?'

'How about anything? You used to tell us what you did. What happened? What's with the secrecy here? What's behind the doors I can't access?'

'We're a government-funded base. There are projects here that we can't talk about with civilians.'

'I'm your father.'

'Yes. And you're a civilian. I understand you want to know things. That's human nature. But we can't talk about a lot of what we do here. There are multiple governments involved. A lot of pieces.'

Harry sighed. 'I get it. You can't tell me anything.'

'Even if I wanted to.' She grinned, trying to pull him back, but he didn't return it. Her grin faded, and a harder edge took over. 'If he can get that chopper in the air today, I suggest you go with him.'

'I said I wouldn't go home without you,' said Harry.

'The fact is, it's against regulations to have civilians staying here,' she said over the top of him.

'I said I wouldn't go home with you,' he repeated, a little louder.

'Obviously, the storm was a mitigating factor,' she said, her own voice rising. 'But now that there's a break, it's time you left.'

'I said I wouldn't go home without you,' he said, almost shouting. People stopped working for a moment to stare at them. Evelyn's face strained into a forced smile to her colleagues, and they quickly lowered their eyes and got back to work. When she turned back to face Harry, the fake smile was a distant memory. Her voice was low, but firm.

'I've known you for all of my life, so don't stand in front of me and pretend that you've never broken a promise to me.'

Harry pulled back a little, before leaning back in. His voice was also low, but firm. 'I'm sorry, did I not come through with that pony I promised to buy?'

'I'm your child, and yet you're acting like one. I'm trying to be professional, okay?'

'Professional?' scoffed Harry. 'Is that what you call keeping that girl here? She needs serious medical attention, not the medieval standard of your fucking infirmary.'

'Spent a lot of time at the hospitals in this part of the world, have you? We know what we're doing. We can look after her.'

Harry frowned. 'Who is she?'

'I already told you,' said Evelyn.

His frown remained. He looked at his daughter's desk. 'What happened to the picture?'

'What picture?' she said, confusion on her face.

'The one of your mother and I. The one you showed the girl. That's how she knew my name, right?'

Evelyn rummaged through the desk. 'I don't know. I must have put it somewhere.'

'Where?' he said. He pushed past her and rifled through her papers carelessly.

'Stop,' she said. 'Those are organised.'

Harry stopped and faced her. 'If things are so organised, then why can't you find the damn picture?'

'Jesus Christ, what's so important about the picture?'

Harry looked at her for a long moment. Finally, he pulled the airline ticket from his pocket and shoved it into her hands. He puffed his chest out, and waited for her to read it.

Evelyn looked at the crumpled ticket. 'What's this?'

'Open it,' he said.

She unfolded it and stared down at the single word written. 'Who wrote this? You?'

'The girl.'

'And?' she said.

'Why is that girl writing down the name of my wife?' said Harry.

She looked at him for a moment, then smiled. Her smile turned into a laugh. 'Oh Dad… You're looking for a conspiracy that doesn't exist.'

Harry ignored her laughter and her belittling tone. 'Why is she writing down your mother's name?'

Evelyn stopped laughing, but the smile remained. 'She was writing down *her* name. She was trying to tell you that her name is Catherine.'

Harry leaned back, already falling from his high place. Already starting to feel like a fool.

'Dad,' she said, 'the government are sending people

for the priest. Serious people. If you're still here once they arrive, it'll be a problem. It'll be a big problem, and I'll be in trouble.'

Harry didn't look at her. He stared off out the window.. For the first time while he had been at the Pyramid, he could see out of it properly.

'Dad…I wish we could have seen each other under better circumstances, but it's time for you to go home. Go home and bury your wife.' She smiled sadly at him, and touched his arm gently for several moments before breaking away and leaving him alone at her desk to stare out the window.

Outside, Bill hosed down the windscreen of his helicopter and prepared to leave, in defiance of the dark clouds that crept at the edges of the horizon.

9

Harry helped Bill load the last of the supplies into the helicopter. They were mostly sealed boxes of research that had to be sent to various government agencies. An old-fashioned technique, though a necessary one ever since the winter had severed communication with the outside world.

'This the last of it?' said Harry.

Bill nodded and wiped sweat from his brow. Even in the cold, it was hard work. 'Yeah, that'll do it. You need to go say your goodbyes?' he said.

Harry looked back at the Pyramid. 'No. No, I'm ready when you are.' He didn't like the way he'd left things with his daughter. He wanted to go back in there and say a proper goodbye, but he also knew he was just as likely to say something that would make them both feel worse. He looked up to the windows, hoping to see her watching him depart. But the sun was peering through the clouds at such an angle that the entire facade of the Pyramid was a reflective surface. He could see the snow and distant mountains in it, distorted at angles. He could see the helicopter, and Bill behind him climbing in and firing it up. He could see his own reflection in the glass. He was twisted at an odd angle. His legs were thin, long branches protruding from the ground.

'Let's get a move on,' barked Bill from behind. He pushed his sunglasses up his red nose, and pulled headphones over his ears as he turned dials and flicked switches on the control board.

Harry took one last look at the high window, before

swinging around and ploughing through the snow to join Bill in the cockpit. He climbed in and buckled up, feeling the machine come to life underneath him. Everything rattled violently, but Bill gave him a reassuring wink and pulled the joystick upward. Harry felt his stomach do a flip, like when he'd drive too fast over a speed bump back home. It was dangerous to think of his car at home, and its warm air conditioner, and the fact that it always stayed firmly on the ground. He thought of this, as the landing skids left the ground, and then returned, and then hovered for a moment before slowly rising. Bill let out a bark of laughter as they began their ascent.

But it didn't last long. There was another rattling sound, this one louder. And this time, when Harry looked across to Bill, he didn't give a cheeky wink, or even a reassuring nod. Without saying anything, Harry knew Bill was thinking 'What the fuck is happening!?' The nose of the helicopter dipped and they fell back to earth. Their fall was only the handful of meters they had climbed, but was a fall nonetheless.

Harry rocked forward in his seat, held in only by the tight belt. When he looked up, he saw something rather extraordinary. Floating in the air above them were the helicopter blades — now broken free of the machine. They spun wildly, and flew across the air for at least forty meters, before they crashed down into the ice.

Bill looked across at Harry. 'You alright?' Harry nodded, he had no words. After a lengthy silence, in which Bill just stared at the blades stuck in the ice, he finally spoke. 'Fuck me blind,' he said.

Harry looked at him, his eyes had lingered on the blades too, but now came back to Bill. 'What happened?'

'Jesus nut… the Jesus nut must have broken,' he said, still looking ahead in bewilderment.

'Jesus nut? What are you saying?' said Harry, unsure if Bill was using a technical term, a prayer or both.

'It's the nut that holds everything together. It's like a thick metal pin that fits in the palm of your hand. They call it that because if it fucks up during a flight, the only thing left is to pray to Jesus.'

Harry looked at Bill incredulously, and even more so when Bill broke into laughter. He laughed so hard, and for so long, that it wore Harry down and eventually he laughed too. He wasn't sure why he was laughing. It wasn't for the joke. More likely for the absurdity he had just witnessed, and for the relief that he was still alive. Though when the laughter faded, all he could think about was the grim reality that he was going to have to leave the hard way. The way he had arrived. On foot.

Later, when Harry and Bill had recovered sufficiently from their near-death experience, they trudged through the snow and slippery ice to retrieve the helicopter blades. It took considerable effort, as they had become wedged in ice, and any thin gap in the surface had since frozen closed in the chill. Harry watched Bill mount the ice and yank at the blades like they were Excalibur in the stone.

By the time the work was done, Harry looked at the horizon and watched the sun settle for the day. Bill was confident he could fix the chopper, but Harry less so. It was a very specific, and important piece. And how it had failed was still a great mystery.

Harry decided he would set out on foot the following morning, weather permitting. It frustrated him that he was inside a high-altitude research facility and not one scientist could tell him the forecast. He was tired of hearing that 'the winters are unpredictable.'

When Harry woke the next morning, the storm had returned tenfold. He stood at the window and stared out once again. Where yesterday he could see clear skies and a far stretch in front of him, now all he saw was snow pounding into the glass. It was the first time that he felt less like a father visiting his daughter, and more like a prisoner of the weather.

Confined to the Pyramid, unable to leave its reach. Again, he thought of home. He thought of the family and friends waiting for him to organise his wife's funeral. He thought about her cold body. He even started to wonder just how long they would wait for him. That's something that never occurred to him before. How long would they wait? Would they go ahead without him? His hand clenched the cheap mobile phone in his pocket. He pulled it out and looked at it. There was zero reception, it had been completely useless since he'd left the capital. He squeezed it tightly in his palm before dropping it into the bin.

10

The Pyramid was abuzz with whispers. Harry had sensed something was happening, even before he started to catch the odd word here and there as the staff traded information. The military were coming. Special forces, if what Harry had overheard was correct. When they would arrive was unclear, and of much debate. Some had expected them the day before, when the weather had been clear. But now with the return of the storm, there was much uncertainty.

Harry noticed that many people seemed on edge. He knew the priest's actions were abhorrent, but he wondered why a special forces team was coming for him, and not just regular law enforcement. Perhaps there was more to the priest than anyone knew, or was letting on. His first thought was to enquire with Evelyn, but he quickly realised that she would no doubt be just as evasive as she had been on every other matter.

Harry checked the bags in his room for the tenth time since breakfast. He was ready to depart and was set on doing so as soon as the smallest break in the storm emerged. Bill had promised to work on repairing the chopper, but Harry didn't think he could afford to wait for that possibility.

He left his room and walked down the brightly lit hallway. In his hands, he carried a woven dreamcatcher. He had taken it from the African man's room. He rounded the corner and knocked on the infirmary door. It pushed open at his touch and he saw that the bed was neatly made. The African man was gone.

The room, however, was not empty. Dr Ming stood

beside the bed, her eyes scanning a chart. 'Hello Harry,' she said as he entered.

Harry looked at her for a moment, then to the empty bed. 'The man, what happened to him?'

'He didn't make it,' she said. 'His wounds became infected, and we just didn't have what we needed to treat him. We were hoping to send Bill out for supplies yesterday, but… well, you know what happened there.' She looked at the dreamcatcher in Harry's hands. 'Was that from his room?'

He took a moment to respond, but then steadied himself. 'Yes. I thought… well I thought it might cheer him up a little. Pointless now,' he said, his voice trailing off.

'That's very kind of you, Harry.'

'Doesn't matter anymore.' Harry put the dream catcher down on the bed. 'What do you know about the military coming here?' he asked, though Ming was clever enough to see through that.

'Probably the same as what you've overheard by the water cooler.' She smiled, looking up from the chart. She closed it and put it on the bedside table. She pushed her glasses up her nose and gave him her full attention. 'Why do you ask?'

'I'm just curious. There's not much else to do around here, in case you hadn't noticed.' She smiled again, but said nothing. Harry pressed a little harder. 'Why all the trouble for one man?'

'One man who killed ten children. He's a dangerous man and this is a dangerous place. You'd think having military on the way would be a comfort.'

'Then why does it seem like everyone is on edge?' said Harry.

She shrugged. 'I haven't been here long enough to know about any of that. You certainly haven't. Besides, your daughter's a scientist, you should know they bristle when the higher-ups come to town. Anything that threatens their research is a problem.'

'Evelyn said me being here would be a problem. That she'd get in trouble.'

'Consider how much money the government sinks into this place. An insane amount. They have a huge stake in what happens here. In all the different projects that are underway. On some more than others. But ask yourself who they send. Maybe a suit? But not in winter. Not when the very act of reaching here can be life and death, as you well know. They send their sled dogs, the military. When they get here, they're basically the eyes and ears of the boss. Do you understand?'

Harry nodded. It was coming to him. 'Yeah, makes sense. Do they know anything more about the priest?'

She shook her head. 'If they do, they haven't told me.'

'Has anyone questioned him since we returned?'

'No. Your daughter insisted that nobody have contact with him. He has a way of twisting words, as well as minds, as you may have seen firsthand'.

Harry smiled bitterly. 'I don't think there's much in his words, or his head for that matter. He's as mad as they come.'

She shivered in the cold, stainless steel room. She picked up the chart from the table, and then looked down upon the dream catcher. Her eyes studied it for a moment. 'Little point in leaving that here now. I'm hoping no one else has need of this bed.'

Harry nodded and picked up the dream catcher. 'Should we send it back to his mother, in Africa?'

'He never supplied us with an address for home. It might take some time to identify his family, and even longer to send word. We'll have to wait until we can get our systems back on track.'

Harry paused thoughtfully, and then had an idea. 'Perhaps I'll leave it in the child's room until then.' He picked up the dream catcher. 'Assuming I'm allowed to see her, and that's not a problem?'

'That should be fine. Just remember last time. Better not to leave any pens laying around.'

Harry smiled and nodded as he left the room.

He gently knocked on the child's door. It was open. He hovered in the doorway for a moment, as her head tilted in his direction. 'Hello Catherine,' he said, and she seemed to recognise his voice at once. He crossed the room in a couple of strides and his eyes roamed for the best place to hang the dream catcher. 'I've brought something for you. It's a dream catcher. They say it wards off evil spirits in your dreams.' He shook it and the beads that hung from lines of string rattled.

She opened her mouth, but no words came, only a wheezing, strangled slur of sounds. She motioned to him for a pen, and he hesitated but only for the briefest of moments. She snatched at the air before finding his hand and taking the pen. She and began scribbling at once. She slid the note across the bedside table and gestured for him to look at it. He reached out and took it in his hand. He stared at it for a moment. It read, 'No dreams.'

'You mean you… don't dream?'

She nodded.

'Here? Or never?'

She didn't answer. In the silence that swam between them, Harry thought about his own dreams and if he had in fact had any in the time he had been at the Pyramid. He'd certainly closed his eyes and caught some small moments of rest… but that rest was punctuated by horrible things. Hands, feet, eyes. Things he pushed down and tried to forget. Though amidst the nightmares, he couldn't for the life of him remember a single dream he'd had. It worried him for a moment, before he shook it off as paranoia. Back home, he could barely remember a dream. Here was no different. He'd spent a few too many days surrounded by people feeding him tales of monsters and insomnia.

Harry stood and looked around the room. He thought he'd finally become used to the chill. He didn't like that. He noticed pictures had been hung on the walls. He looked back sadly at the child, whose eyes were gone and whose face was covered by a cloth. She would never see these pictures again. He looked at them. There were four, one for each corner. They were all of trees. Harry smiled. 'My daughter must be behind this,' he said to the child, over his shoulder. 'She always loved trees.'

He crossed the room and sat back down beside her bed. 'It surprised me when she said she was coming to work here. I never thought a place like this would appeal to her, so high up in the mountains, no trees in sight.' Harry sat in quiet contemplation for a moment. 'I think the last tree I saw would have been several days down the mountain.'

The child stirred. She tried to speak again, but the pain still won out, so she scribbled her thought down on paper and held it up for him to see. It read, 'I like trees too.'

Harry nodded. 'My wife was the same. She had that in common with Evelyn.' He smiled at the thought. 'We had this huge property in the country. It was just our house for miles on all sides. A full garden. A lake we would never let Evelyn go near, because we never knew how deep it was. But close by the house was this giant oak tree. It was beautiful. In the mornings, you could look out the window from the kitchen table and see the sun breaking through the branches at the top. We were on a hill, so those branches would cop a fair blast of wind. But that tree was strong. It had these thick branches like arms. And I remember all that Evelyn ever wanted was a swing on that tree. She would ask about it all the time. And one day I relented and I told her that I would build her one. I said it almost as a throwaway line, but she would never forget anything, that girl. She'd remember the tiniest details, and she came to me every morning and would say "Is the swing finished yet, Daddy? Is the swing finished yet, Daddy?" She must have been about eight years old, and she would just ask and ask and ask every day. But finally, I finished it. This little red seat, and her sitting on it. It's funny how something so simple could take her away for so many hours at a time.' Harry stared off for a long time.

The child smiled, and the only sound in the room was the occasional beep of her monitor. The reminiscent glint in Harry's eye faded, and was replaced by something harder.

'We lost that swing, and the tree, and the house too. Fire ripped through it one summer,' he said. 'She used to call that tree her safe place. But it was gone.'

The smile had left the child's face too. She scratched on her paper and held it for Harry to see. It read, 'Not safe.'

Harry shook his head at her, confused. 'What do you mean?'

'Here,' she said aloud, her throat aching and her small voice barely a croaky whisper. 'Here, not safe.' Her head tilted back in her pillow, exhausted from the effort of stringing a mere few words together.

'I don't understand,' said Harry.

She leaned forward again. 'Coming… here,' she managed.

'Who?' said Harry, sorry that he had to drag agonising words from her.

'Soldiers,' she said. 'Bad… men. We… go.'

'How? We're trapped.'

She slammed her hand down hard on the bedside table in front of him. When she removed it, Harry saw the Jesus nut. The crucial, missing piece from the helicopter. 'We… fly,' she said.

Harry took the nut in his hand. 'You took it? How?'

She shook her head, as if none of that mattered. 'Go… please… help… me.' She took his hand in hers and squeezed it tight. It warmed Harry. He stood, and let go of her hands.

'I'm going to find the pilot. We're going to fix the helicopter. I'm going to get you out of here.'

'P-promise,' she stammered.

'I promise,' he said, and he swept from the room.

11

Harry snaked down the hallway. He avoided the gaze of all he passed. Dr Ming smiled at him, but it went unreturned. He was a man on a mission. With the helicopter nut clenched firmly in his hand, he bounded towards the outside. He pushed through the heavy doorway and into the main hall. Evelyn glanced up from her computer screen to see him heading for the door, but quickly got back to her work.

Harry stopped by the clear window. Outside the storm continued, as it had for almost all his time there. He could just see the outline of the helicopter near the edge of the facility. A feint shadow moved around the base of it. Harry smiled as he watched Bill battle the storm, all in the effort of making repairs. He smiled further still, as he knew what he held in his hand was the missing link.

He dragged the heavy front doors open and was nearly knocked down by the wind. He steadied and marched towards Bill.

'Hey!' he screamed in his direction. Bill turned to face him. 'Jesus nut,' said Harry with a grin. He held the nut up in the air, and he could see Bill's eyes squinting at it until he too grinned.

Harry heard the whistle only seconds before he felt the heat of the flames. The helicopter in front of him was engulfed by a fireball, and Bill cooked along with it. The roaring wind was drowned out by a pulsating ringing in his ears, and everything around him slowed.

Out of the fire, Bill staggered forwards. Half his face

had melted off into the snow, and if Harry could have heard anything but the ringing, it would have been Bill's agonised screams. He collapsed mere meters from Harry's feet, his flaming body smoldering in the ice it lay upon. Harry sank to his knees and reached out a hand to help, but knew that there was no help he could give.

Harry looked around helplessly. The Pyramid's windows were a sea of concerned faces as people looked out on the wreckage. Harry held their gaze for a moment, but then stared out into the darkness. He squinted, sensing, rather than seeing something. He looked for long enough that a small dot of light appeared on the edge of his vision. It was joined by another on the left, then another on the right. Soon there were a dozen small lights, and they grew bigger as they drew closer.

Harry stood up. His knees shook, but he moved backwards towards the door of the Pyramid. Before he reached it, a tingle ran down his spine as he heard another whistle. It swirled through the air and grew louder as it approached. This time, he saw it. He watched the rocket collide with the fiery wreckage of the helicopter, and watched it climb in the air with a fireball underneath it. Harry's eyes lingered on what remained of Bill's body, as he slipped on the ground. He clambered for the door and huddled for safety inside.

'Close the door,' said Evelyn, rushing towards him.

'What the fuck is going on!?' screamed Harry, his ears still ringing from the explosion.

'Move,' said Evelyn, pushing Harry aside and sliding a heavy bolt across the doorway, locking it. 'They're here.'

'Who?' said Harry.

'Soldiers.'

'Why are they shooting at us? Why the fuck did they kill Bill?'

She ignored him, and inspected the thick door. 'This will slow them down.' But she fell backwards immediately as the door was hammered from the outside.

'Stand back,' screamed a muffled voice from outside.

Evelyn climbed to her feet and looked around at her colleagues. 'Don't worry. They wouldn't risk damaging the facility.' The end of her sentence was drowned out by another hammer against the door.

Harry strained his ears, and could hear muffled movement from outside, followed by one final warning cry. 'Stand back.'

Harry scurried backwards, dragging Evelyn with him, but they were knocked from their feet as an explosion shook the foundations of the control room.

Smoke rose from the doorway. The hammering resumed, but quick work was made of it. With one final strike, the heavy door creaked forwards, slowly at first, then all at once as it slammed into the floor. The smoke around the doorway cleared, and standing in it were a dozen heavily-equipped soldiers.

Evelyn seized Dr Ming by the arm and dragged her close. 'Go quickly. Secure the research,' she whispered. Ming nodded and made for the other door, but a booming voice stopped her.

'If anyone leaves this room, they die,' said a man as he stepped forward. He aimed a gun at Ming, and she meekly fell back in with the crowd. He walked further into the room, his men followed. They left a gaping hole in the door behind them, and already drops of snow had begun sneaking in. The man, clearly their leader looked around at all the faces. 'Where is Dr Martin?' he said.

Nobody answered. Finally, Evelyn stepped forward.

'He's dead,' she said.

The man turned to face her. He stood in front of her, and looked down his crooked nose at her. His hair was white like the snow, but flecked with grey, and his eyes were beady like a rat's. 'How did he die?'

'Do you really care?'

He smiled down at her. 'No. I suppose I don't. Are you in charge?'

She nodded.

'Who are you?'

'Dr Bell.'

He holstered his firearm. 'Well, Dr Bell, I'm Colonel Grant.'

'Colonel?' she asked, surprised.

'That's right,' he said.

'We'd previously dealt with a captain.'

'The captain died fighting a war. While you monkeys chased bananas in this pyramid.'

Evelyn smiled. 'I see you have his bedside manner.'

Grant's hand rested on his holster. He returned her smile, but none of it reached his narrow eyes.

'My men and I don't really care for the jibes of lab coats, Dr Bell. You ought to know that. Can I hazard a guess that Dr Martin died roughly six weeks ago?'

Evelyn said nothing. There was a deathly silence around the entire room.

Grant smiled. 'Right about the time we lost communications with this base. Convenient.'

'You'll find, Colonel, that it has been very far from convenient for us,' said Evelyn.

Grant leaned in closer to her, his voice was lower but still carried over the wind for all to hear. 'And if I have my men inspect the wires here, they'll find them in perfect order, will they? Or will they find some clumsy fool hacked at them with a kitchen knife and pair of scissors?' He nodded for his man to open the circuit box. The soldier crossed the room in a few steps and wrenched it open. All eyes shifted to see a mess of coloured wires, cut to pieces. Harry looked at Evelyn, but she avoided his gaze.

'We don't know anything about that. It could have been the mad priest for all we know.'

'Where is the priest?' asked Grant.

'In a holding room.'

'Good. We'll deal with him later. As for now, I want to see it.'

Evelyn hesitated for a moment. 'You can't.'

Grant stopped glancing around the room and looked straight at her. He spoke again, but slower. 'I want to see it.'

'It's not working,' she said.

'I don't care.'

'It's broken.'

'I don't care.' There was a finality in his voice. 'Take me to it now.'

Evelyn looked around at her colleagues. Their faces were all as dark as hers. Harry watched her hands shake at her sides, and stepped forward before he knew what words were going to spill from his mouth. He hadn't even begun to speak before half a dozen guns were pointed at every inch of him.

'You just burned a man alive,' he said.

'Who the fuck are you?' said Grant, pointing a handgun in his direction.

'His fucking face melted off, you son of a bitch.'

Grant stepped forward and pushed the barrel of the gun against Harry's temple.

'A man with a gun is asking you who the fuck you are.'

'I'm… I'm,' began Harry.

'He's nobody,' said Evelyn stepping in front of him. 'He's a stray, lost in the storm. He came in a few days ago.'

Grant looked Harry up and down. 'Get rid of him.'

'What do you want us to do, throw him out in the storm?'

'I don't care what you do. We don't pay you to house civilians.'

'This civilian is the one who found the priest. Out in the storm. He stopped him and brought him back here. He did your job for you.'

'My job?' said Grant.

'It's your job to protect us, no?' said Evelyn.

'And what about your job? To send us reports. What about that?' When she didn't respond, he smiled wider.

'I want to see it,' he said as he turned his back on her and proceeded towards the heavy locked door that led below. His men followed him.

Evelyn touched Harry's arm, and lowered her voice. 'You're not my father,' she said without looking at him.

'What?' he said, bewildered.

'You're not my father, okay? Trust me.' She glanced sideways and made eye contact with him briefly.

'I'll come see you, once I'm done with them.' She swept from the room to join the Colonel.

12

Harry sat on his bed and waited for his daughter to arrive. Once she did, he was sure she would straighten everything out. He was sure she would fill him in on all the answers to the countless questions he had. She'd tell him why the wires were cut. Why the military had blown up their helicopter and stormed the base. And why she was suddenly working for soldiers. He knew nothing.

A wave of relief washed over him when he finally heard a knock on the door. He leapt from the bed, across the room to the door in a couple of strides and wrenched it open. What greeted him on the other side, however, was not his daughter.

'Evening,' said Colonel Grant. He held a bottle of whisky in one hand, and swayed on the spot ever so slightly. 'Mind if I…' he began, but waltzed in before he'd finished his sentence. He looked around the small room and grimaced. 'Not much, is it? You can close that door.' Harry looked out into the hallway, before closing the door. Grant looked him up and down again. 'What's your handle?'

'Harry,' he said.

'We got off on the wrong foot, Harry,' said Grant as he took a seat atop the small desk beside the bed. He swigged from the whisky bottle. 'Brave thing you did, taking down the priest.'

'Anyone would have.'

'No, I've seen men with training resist the call when it's their time. What you did was no small feat.' He swigged from the bottle again, then offered it to Harry who refused with a polite shake of his head. 'You need something to warm you out here.'

'We were warm enough, before you blew the door down. And before you murdered the pilot.'

'I'm doing my job. Don't let the short time you've spent with these noble scientists cloud your judgement.'

'I don't know enough about this place to even have a proper judgement.'

Grant swigged again. 'That's a good thing, Harry. You don't want to know a thing about this place. The mad priest. He found out, and look at him now.' A silence hung in the space between them, broken only by another swig from the fast emptying bottle.

Harry cleared his throat. 'You've talked to him then, the priest?'

Grant laughed. But it was a bitter sound. 'Yeah, I have. Why do you think I need to fucking drink?'

'What did he say?' said Harry.

'Only the same thing, over and over.'

Harry didn't need to ask what it was. He already knew. 'They do not fear, they cannot hear. They do not feel, they are not real. They cannot see, they should not be.' He finished softly, staring away from Grant.

'Are you sure you don't need a drink?' said Grant with a smirk.

Harry shook his head. 'A drink won't make me forget.'

'Well, one won't.' Grant shook the nearly empty bottle. 'Why do you think he came back?'

'I couldn't figure that out,' said Harry. 'Perhaps to finish what he started.'

Grant put the bottle down.

'That's a sobering thought.' He looked at Harry for a smile, but found none. 'You're a grim fucker, aren't you Harry? That priest won't be finishing anything, not without help at least.'

'You think I'd help him?'

'No, I don't. It's the scientists I'd worry about. You can't trust any of them.'

'Why not?'

'Because all they ever do is come up with theories, and run tests, and do everything they can for the *future of the world*. They don't give a shit about this world that the rest of us live in.' He picked up the bottle again and took a small sip, not wanting to finish it. 'They tell me you're a history teacher.'

Harry nodded.

Grant continued, 'The thing about history is that it shows you all the ways we did it wrong, if you're smart enough to listen. You can learn everything there is about warfare from those who have come before us. Science is the thing you can't control. Think about the history of humanity, Harry. Soldiers fight wars. Scientists end them. We're in the trench, while they build a bomb.' Grant slumped a little in his seat, but he persisted, 'I've seen more kids die than I can stand to remember. Their eyes flicker and fade like a gaslight in the trenches. But when you get to the bottom of it,' he drained the last of the whiskey, 'we're just tainted meat for crows.'

He stood, swaying slightly, and made for the door. Harry stood aside to let him pass. As he opened the door, he was greeted by a face.

'Colonel Grant?' said Evelyn.

'Ah, Dr Bell. We were just having a conversation about science, and all the wonderful, important work you do.' Grant crossed the room and collected his empty whisky bottle.

'I'll get out of your hair now.' He lingered in the doorway, turning back to face them. 'I don't want to get in the way of father–daughter time.' He smiled, as they both failed to hide the surprise on their faces.

Grant nodded towards Harry. 'I'll be seeing you, Harry Bell.' He tipped the empty bottle in Harry's direction, before turning on his heel and walking away. Harry listened to his footsteps until long after they had rounded the corner, and then closed the door.

'You have to leave,' said Evelyn.

'He's a mad man,' said Harry.

'He's dangerous. He knows who you are. What you are to me.'

'Stop, Evelyn. Just tell me what the hell all of this is about. What are you doing for them? Why are they threatening you?'

'I can't talk about it.'

'I don't give two shits about it being classified.'

She held an envelope in her hand. 'Take it,' she said, but he didn't move.

'What is it?'

'Money.'

'What are you doing?'

She thrust it into his hands. 'It's twenty thousand dollars. Take it outside, and pay off one of the soldiers guarding their snowmobiles. Take one, get through the storm and get the hell as far away from here as you can.'

'Come with me.'

'I want to try and fix the world, Dad. I can't fix the world if I run away.'

'The world isn't broken, Evelyn. People are.'

She looked at him and smiled. 'You'll never be safe here. Not with me. I've put you in danger by allowing you to stay this long.'

'You were protecting me from the storm,' he said.

'Yes. But now Grant's here.'

'Let me help you, whatever trouble you're in.'

'The best way to help is to leave. You're my only weakness.' She put her hand on his and squeezed it tight. 'Take the money, and get far away. For me.'

Harry bit his lip and hesitated.

'Are you going to be okay?' He looked at her for a long time, but she didn't answer.

13

To Harry's relief, the soldiers were either sleeping or otherwise occupied. When he reached the doorway to the main hall, he dumped his bag beside it. He reached out for the door handle, but found it locked. The key card scanner beside it lit up red, denying him entry. He had expected Grant to take measures to keep people from leaving through the gaping hole left in the building.

He rolled back his sleeve and checked his watch. He turned and marched away from his bag, and back down below.

He raised his hand to knock on the door, but realised the time for courtesy was over, and he wished to be as silent as possible. He swept into the room, and the child raised her head at the sound of his arrival.

'Harry?' she croaked.

'That's right, it's me,' he said crossing the room in two steps and taking her hand. 'I'm ready to check out of here, how about you?'

She smiled. 'Helicopter?'

'No, no I'm afraid not,' said Harry as he helped her sit up. He wrapped the blanket around her shoulders. 'It's going to be very cold.'

'The soldiers… the helicopter?'

'That's right. Don't worry about them.'

'Came here.' She coughed. 'Questions.'

'There won't be any more questions. I promise you.' He helped her put shoes on, and then climb down from the bed. 'Let's go,' he said, just as the door behind them opened.

Dr Ming entered. Her head was buried in a notebook, but she dropped it in surprise when she looked up. 'What are you doing?' she said.

'We're leaving,' said Harry. 'Dr Ming… I need you to step away from the door.'

Ming didn't move an inch. 'Do you have any idea what they'll do to you? Both of you?'

'Please move,' he said.

'You can't take her,' she said, looking at the girl. 'She's too important.'

Harry looked from Ming to the child, and back. 'I don't know what the hell goes on in this place. I know you're not studying altitude or the weather. I hear whispers of tests, and monsters, and all sorts of shit… But I know one thing for sure, Doctor, and it's that you don't agree with it. You know they're wrong. You know you're not safe. You know that.'

Ming shivered in the open doorway. She looked at him for a long moment. When she spoke, her voice was low, and it shook more than her hands. 'They'll kill me.'

Harry squeezed the child's arm tight, before crossing the room to stand in front of Ming. 'Come with us. We'll use your key to get through. I've paid off a soldier. We can all make it out of here.'

'Into the storm?' said Ming.

'Which would you rather?' he said.

She nodded a yes, and kept nodding as if to convince herself. 'I only ever wanted what was best for the children,' she said. 'Everything else was noise.'

They crept along the corridor, thankful that the soldiers were asleep. Ming stopped them at every turn, so that she could go first and make sure the coast was clear. When they reached the doorway to the main hall they stopped to breathe. Harry collected his bag and threw it over his back. Ming swiped her key card, and the light turned green, allowing them entry. They held their breath as the doors opened, and let out a collective sigh when they saw the main hall was empty. There was nothing between them and the exit. The noise of the storm outside drifted into the room, courtesy of the hole the soldiers had blown in the front of the building.

Harry hurried them across the room and through the hole. 'Quickly, we're almost there,' he said.

'Where's the guard you paid off?' asked Ming, as she ducked through the hole.

'He'll meet us by the snowmobiles. It's not far.'

They shuffled through snow and made their way around the edge of the Pyramid, not far from where the helicopter once lay. A burly soldier had his back to them, he stood before a dozen snowmobiles, half covered in fresh snowfall. He turned to face them, and his smug face curled into a scowl. It was impossible to judge his physique under the five layers of clothing he wore.

'What the fuck is this? Three people?' he shouted at Harry, looking from him to Ming, and then the child. 'You didn't say nothing about three.'

Harry stepped in close to him. 'Keep your voice down,' he said.

'Who gives a shit,' spat the soldier. 'Nobody's going to hear a thing over the wind.' He shoved Harry back, hard. 'You didn't tell me there'd be three. That changes things.'

'You want more money?' said Harry.

'Fuck yes, I do.'

'How much?'

'Double,' said the soldier with a grin.

Harry put his hand in his pocket and pulled a roll of notes. 'Fine.' He stuffed the money into the soldier's hand. 'We have a deal.' The soldier smirked, happy with his score. Harry smirked too. He'd had the foresight to only use half of Evelyn's money when he dealt with the soldier earlier. He had anticipated trouble, and was right.

The soldier moved through the snow and slapped a hand down on one of the snowmobiles. 'This is it,' he said. 'It's got a full tank, and should get you far enough. Visibility will be dog shit, but that's not my problem.'

'What's all this then,' came a voice from behind. They turned to see another soldier walk slowly towards them. His hand rested on his holster.

'Captain… They came out for a smoke, was just telling them to get back inside,' lied the soldier, giving Harry a push.

'The colonel said nobody was allowed outside. Nobody,' said the captain. His eyes took in Harry and Ming, and finally they worked their way down to the child. He looked at the bandages around her eyes. The slash across her throat. His mouth hung open. His hand shook as he lifted it and pointed towards her. 'That's the kid. What the fuck is going on? She can't be out here.'

'I know,' said the soldier, stepping forward to placate him. 'I know.'

'She's too important. Do you know how much trouble we'll be in?'

'It's alright, okay?' said the soldier. 'We'll figure it out.'

The captain looked at Harry and Ming. 'We have to kill them.'

The words carried to Harry, who stiffened at once. 'We had a deal,' he shouted at the soldier.

'You shut your mouth,' he barked, looking back at Harry. 'I'm handling this.'

'What do you mean you're handling this?' the captain asked him. 'You cut a deal? You're as dead as they are.' He pushed the soldier away from him and drew his gun. The soldier reached for it and the two men wrestled clumsily for control of the weapon. The captain wrenched a hand free and swung the grip of the gun down hard on the soldier's head, cutting him and sending him to the ground. 'The colonel will deal with you, traitor,' he spat. He walked towards Harry and Ming, the gun in his hand rising level with their heads.

Harry stepped in front of Ming and the child. He held his hands up in surrender. 'You don't have to do this.'

The captain stopped and looked at him with pity. 'You don't understand a thing. This is the only thing I can do.' He aimed the gun at them. His hand shook. 'I don't have a choice.' He looked at the child. 'Come here, girl.'

Harry put a hand on the child's shoulder. 'You're not touching her. She's suffered enough.'

The captain shook his head. 'You don't get it. She's going to live. It's you and the doctor who die. Either that, or you all can… Come here now, girl.' Behind him, the soldier quietly rose to his feet. He seized the captain from behind and wrenched the gun from his grasp. It landed in the snow between them and Harry.

Harry charged forward to help, scooping up the gun,

and removing the clip. He seized the captain's shoulders to wrench him off the soldier.

The captain swung a wild hand around and struck Harry in the face. He dropped the gun, and the captain kicked free of the soldier and dived for it. 'I'll fucking kill all of you,' he snarled like a rabid dog, spit flying from his panting mouth.

'You're outnumbered,' said Harry.

'I have a gun,' he said, aiming it at Harry.

Harry smiled at him. 'I took the clip out.'

The captain faltered a moment. He turned the gun over in his hand to inspect the missing clip. He smirked. 'Still one left in the chamber, you dumb fuck.'

It was Harry's turn to falter. 'Well, you can hardly shoot all of us,' he said, knowing he was probably to be the unlucky one.

'No, not all of you,' said the captain. 'Just her.' He pointed through them, at the child. 'I'd sooner see her dead than in your hands.' He aimed the gun at her. She stood perfectly still. The only movement came from Ming, who sprinted forward to stand in front of the child. 'Move,' barked the captain.

Ming shook her head. 'No,' she said. 'I'm not moving.'

'Move,' he said again, louder.

'No,' she repeated. 'I'm tired of doing nothing.'

'Last chance,' he said. The muscles in his face tensed, as she failed to respond. His finger twitched on the trigger. When he spoke again, the words exploded from his mouth with venom. 'Fucking move!' She didn't. His finger did. The gunshot sounded like a cough against the wind. The bullet tore through Ming's chest. She fell backwards, her fall broken by the child.

'Hold him,' shouted Harry to the soldier, who laid a tackle on the captain. Harry slid across the snow to reach Ming. He held her head up in his hands. He readied himself to tell her that everything was going to be okay, that they would get help, that he could make everything right. But he took one look at the hole in her chest and the blood that had already stained the snow, and his entire body shook with helplessness. There was nothing he could do.

'Close your eyes,' he said. He thought of putting pressure on the wound, but saw no point. Instead he took her shaking hand and held it tight. 'Close your eyes,' he said again. She looked up at him helplessly for a moment. Her eyes were wild and panicked. She did as he asked and closed them. He held her hand, tighter still. 'Close your eyes, and think of home.' He and child sat with her for several moments, before she slipped away.

In the silence, he heard words. 'They do not fear, they cannot hear. They do not feel, they are not real. They cannot see, they should not be.'

Harry looked around. The words came from the captain. He struggled in the tight headlock of the soldier. Harry stood up and walked towards him, Ming's blood still dripping from his hands. The captain repeated the words. 'They do not fear, they cannot hear. They do not feel, they are not real. They cannot see, they should not be.'

Harry stood over him now. 'Let him go,' he said to the soldier, who let his grip slide and stood up out of the way. Harry's attention turned to the captain. 'Why are you saying that?' The captain looked at him, without expression, but said nothing. 'Where did you hear that?' said Harry, now in his face.

The captain looked from Harry to the child, before repeating the words. 'They do not fear, they cannot hear. They do not feel, they are not real. They cannot see, they should not be.' When he finished, he stared into the darkness.

Harry clenched his fist, as his rage built. He lifted a foot and brought his heavy boot down hard on the captain's face, knocking him out.

A long silence followed, which was broken by the soldier. 'Take your snowmobile and get the fuck out of here.' He looked down on at the unconscious body of the captain in front of him. He felt the blood on his head, as though just discovering it. He looked at Harry, but his eyes were glazed. He put a hand out into the air, as if to grab a hold of something, but there was nothing to hold, so he dropped to his knees. 'I just need…' he said, leaning back until he was seated in the snow. 'Head's spinning. I just need to sit down for a minute.'

Harry looked at Ming, and then the child and the snowmobile that sat waiting behind her. It was all right there. But something nagged at him. *The words.* The damn words the captain had uttered. The same words he'd heard from the mad priest. The words swam around in his head, and he realised he'd been standing still for several minutes. He shook his head, before smiling. 'Damn fool,' he said under his breath. He tossed the gun clip into the snow, and turned to face the seated soldier. 'I need to go back for something.' But the soldier was passed out. Exhaustion, or perhaps concussion claiming him.

Harry turned to the child and crouched down in front of her. 'I have to go back in. I have to talk to the priest. I… I have to know what the words are. What this place is. I just have to know.' He placed a reassuring hand on her arm. 'I'll be quick. I just can't leave without knowing.'

Harry turned away, leaving her alone with the motionless bodies. He neared the hole in the front of the building. Behind him, the child clambered through the snow and blood, until her hands touched upon the cold metal of a gun.

14

The security key card was splattered with Ming's blood. Harry tried to ignore it as he slid the card into the reader and the red light turned green. He opened the door and saw the priest. He was sitting at a table. His hands were tied with rope and chain. No chances were taken. The skin around his wrists was chaffed, his lips were cracked and his ragged clothes hung to his slight frame. He'd looked far bigger with a knife in his hand, Harry thought as he closed the door behind him. The priest looked up at the sound. His eyes focused on Harry and his cracked lips stretched into a smile. Harry waited for him to speak, but he didn't.

'Half expected you to still be muttering to yourself,' said Harry. 'Why did you come back?'

The priest shifted in his seat, as much as he could. 'I would ask you the same thing,' he said. 'But I already know the answer.'

'Why did you want to come back here?' said Harry again, a little louder.

'You know why.'

'Because you're not finished,' said Harry. 'What makes you think you can finish anything from in here?'

'Faith.'

'Faith in what?'

'You.' The priest smiled wider. His cracked lips parted, revealing blood-stained teeth.

Harry shook his head, confused. 'I don't understand.'

'I had faith that you would help me. That you'd help me, once you found out.'

'I haven't found out anything.'

'And that's why you came back. You had a sniff of freedom, but something clawed at you with its fingernails and pulled you back.'

Harry shifted uncomfortably. He eyed the door for a moment, then looked back at the priest. 'What makes you think I was outside?'

The priest nodded to Ming's card, still clutched in Harry's hand.

He glanced at the door. 'Followed here?'

'They're all asleep,' said Harry.

'Not all. There's always someone awake here.' He looked around the small room that had been his home for days. 'Here's okay. It's below you need to worry about.' He stared down, through the floor. His head tilted forward and his eyes glazed. He just stared down for so long that Harry felt uncomfortable in the silence.

'Are there monsters down there?' said Harry.

The priest's eyes snapped up from the floor and bored into Harry. 'There're monsters everywhere.'

'What is this place?' said Harry, but it went unanswered. 'What's down there?'

'They do not fear, they cannot hear. They do not feel, they are not real. They cannot see, they should not be,' he said, with a smile bordering on madness.

Harry stepped forward and slammed his fist on the table. 'Tell me what it is.'

The priest leaned in close enough that Harry could smell the rotten breath that passed through his stained teeth. 'I'll show you. I'll show you what I saw. I know the way. You have the key,' he nodded to Ming's bloodied card.

Harry didn't even hesitate. He cut him free of the table, but left his hands bound. He wrenched him up. The priest hadn't walked in days and his weak knees buckled, but the table stopped him from falling. 'Can you walk?' said Harry, standing over him.

The priest looked at Harry, standing so close by him. 'You're not afraid of me like the others.'

'If you were going to kill me, you'd have done it by now. Move,' said Harry, prodding him hard in the back.

They moved quietly down the hallway. They reached a sealed door at the end. A card scanner glowed red beside it. The priest nodded towards the card, and Harry scanned it. The red glow remained for a moment, then turned green. The heavy doors parted in the middle to reveal an elevator. Harry pushed the priest inside and quickly followed.

'Which button,' he asked, noticing there were several, and all of them unmarked.

The priest didn't even look at them. 'Doesn't matter,' he said. 'They all go to the same place.'

'How far down is it?'

'Far,' he said, before his eyes unfocused and he began muttering the words under his breath. Again, and again. Then he cleared his throat. 'Where's your wife?' he said, abruptly.

Harry was momentarily stunned by the question. He wondered why that had come up. He wondered if someone, a guard or a scientist perhaps, had told the priest about his wife for some reason. He gathered himself. 'She's dead,' he said.

'Have you said a prayer?'

'Would your God be listening?' said Harry.

'Perhaps not…' said the priest, trailing off.

Harry returned to wondering how absurdly far down they were going. He began to reach for the button again, in the hope that hitting one might bring their descent to an end. But then the priest's voice interrupted his train of thought.

'He listened to me,' he said.

'What?' said Harry, confused, and playing catch-up with the madman.

'God listened to me.'

Harry smirked. 'When was that? When you butchered those children?'

'When my wife and son died,' he said. 'My son loved to draw. He always had paper and a pencil at hand. Sometimes we'd go on Sunday drives. My friends would mock me for that, that I had become so domesticated. So normal. So boring. But there's nothing boring about being happy. My wife would often sit in the back seat with him. She'd be on hand to pass him pencils, like a surgical assistant. But on this day, she was tired and resting her eyes. My boy held up a picture. I can still hear his voice now, begging me to look at it, to look at what he'd created. I turned around and I looked at the picture, and then I looked at him. Then my ears filled with the sound of a horn, and bent metal, and broken glass, and everything else that followed when the truck split our car in half.' He stared so intensely that Harry had to look away.

The priest continued, 'I climbed out of the wreckage. I stepped through broken glass that had the pieces of my whole world splattered on it. And I stood before a church. It all happened in front of a church. The way I saw it, I had two choices. I could burn it to the ground, or I could walk inside, kneel and listen for an answer.'

Harry shivered in the silence that followed, until he spoke, 'Did you get an answer?'

The priest looked at him for a long moment. 'I still carry the picture.' He looked up at Harry's confused expression. 'My boy's drawing. I carry it everywhere.' He reached into his jacket and pulled out a tattered, folded piece of paper. Faded blood stained the frayed edges. 'It reminds me that we have no control. But God does. Do you want to see it?'

Harry didn't, but it was shoved in his direction all the same. He slowly unfolded it. There was a ding and finally the elevator doors opened, revealing a bright green haze. Harry squinted in the light, as he watched the priest silently shuffle out of the elevator. Harry looked down at the drawing. It was a car crash; a truck splitting a car in half. The driver's eyes were wide open, while a pair of x's marked the eyes of the woman and boy in the back seat. One word was scrawled in the corner of the page, *Goodbye*.

Harry watched the priest wander into the haze. He folded the drawing up, and followed him.

The haze obscured Harry's view. He could see shiny surfaces, like those in rooms above. But everything was cast in a ghostly green hue. Dozens of shelves held hundreds of small glass vials. Their transparent green contents held in place by corks. Thick pipes ran along the floor and snaked their way around the walls and ceiling. Harry's eyes followed them down the long room and saw that they connected to a series of tanks.

As he stepped closer, he realised that the walls were lined with hundreds of tanks. They were upright and filled with the same material as the vials, only here, they bubbled away. It was the only sound that crept through the room, other than the slow footsteps of he and the priest.

'What is this?' he called out, his voice barely rising above a whisper. Harry noticed clouds of mist spill from his mouth, suddenly aware of the frigid cold. Harry stepped up in front of a tank. His breath fogged the glass. He reached out and wiped away the condensation, to reveal a face. He stumbled backwards. 'They're people,' he stammered, unable to keep his voice down. He took another step in and stared into the next tank, and the next, and the one after that.

'They're children… They're all children.' He turned to face the priest, and found him standing right behind him.

'They do not fear, they cannot hear,' he began, pushing past Harry and walking closer to the tanks. 'They do not feel, they are not real.' He reached out and ran his fingers along the glass. 'They cannot see, they should not be.' His whole hand rested on the glass, covering the eyes of a child. He began his chant again.

'Stop,' said Harry.

But the priest continued.

'I said stop,' he said, a little louder.

The priest turned to face him. His eyes were wild. 'They do not feel, they are not real.'

'I said fucking stop!' Harry roared.

The priest lifted his voice to match. 'They cannot see, they should not be!'

Harry lunged at him, grabbing a fistful of his shirt and dragging him away from the tanks. The priest continued to chant, his speech ragged. Harry threw him to the ground. 'I'm warning you to shut your fucking mouth,' said Harry.

But the priest looked at him, and his wild expression had faded, replaced now with confusion. The next sound to leave his mouth was not a repeated chant, but a scream. It came from deep within him. Up from his stomach, through his windpipe, and escaping out into the world where it would never be caught. He screamed and screamed, and when his breath should have run out and his voice should have failed, he somehow carried on screaming.

Harry watched in complete shock as the priest's limbs flailed about. He writhed on the ground as if he was possessed. The screaming never ceased. He clawed at his clothing, as if the pain came from within. Once he'd torn that away, his hands didn't hesitate to tear at the skin that stood between him and the pain that must be stopped. His skin stuck under his nails, and his chest looked as if a rabid beast had slashed at it. But somewhere between the screaming and the tearing and the impossible pain, the priest's heart had given up. His arms dropped to his side. His head rolled back. His eyes, that had bulged so wide as if to escape his head, remained open as his life ended.

Harry sank to the floor. He breathed heavily in the cold. He looked at the twisted body of the priest before him, and he shook in the silence.

'Hello?' called a soft voice from the dark.

Harry spun around in fright and scrambled backwards. 'Who's there?' he said.

'Who… who's that?' said the soft voice. A shadow grew in the haze.

Harry tensed as it grew close. It was a boy. A ginger-haired, small boy. He was naked, and dripping in something that still clung to his skin.

'Where am I?' he said, with an unmistakable Irish accent. He looked at the dead body of the priest beside Harry, and shivered. 'Who's that?' He looked around the room. 'What is this place?'

Before Harry could answer, a deep voice cut through the darkness. 'It didn't work,' it said. The next sound was a click. And then a bang. Harry watched in horror as a hole exploded in the boy's head, and the boy's body collapsed forward to join the dead priest on the floor.

Colonel Grant stepped into the light, shaking his head at the bodies before him. 'Fucking waste,' he said, spitting at the ground. He holstered his gun.

Harry tried desperately to form words, but couldn't. His plight became harder when a second person stepped into the light. It was Evelyn.

'Dad,' she said. 'I wanted you to be far away from here.'

'What… what have you done?' said Harry, his words shook as much as his body. He pointed to all the other tanks, and the bodies.

'Clones,' she said, as casually as if discussing the weather. 'We've farmed clones.'

Harry looked into her steady face for a moment, before emptying his stomach on the ground. He rolled over and coughed it all up on the floor, where some of it mixed with the blood of the ginger boy.

'Fuck's sake,' said Grant. 'What did I say about civilians? Pull yourself together.' He seized Harry by the scruff of the neck, and wrenched him to his feet. He looked at the sick that dribbled down Harry's chin and shook his head in disgust. He pushed Harry away, and Harry staggered towards the tanks to see the ghostly faces of more sleeping children.

Harry turned back to the priest, and the small ginger boy who lay atop him. 'That's the priest… and the… and the priest?' he said.

Evelyn nodded. 'That's right.'

'How?' said Harry.

'It's complicated.'

Harry stared at the green faces. 'Why are they all so young?'

Evelyn hesitated to respond, but Grant did it for her.

'Because your daughter had one job, and she fucked it,' he said.

Evelyn swung around to face him. 'My job was to make it possible. We're still working out the *kinks*.'

Grant laughed. But it was forced, and bitter. 'Kinks… We've sunk a fortune into this place, and what we get is *kinks*.'

'What you need is patience,' she fired back.

'Patience?' said Grant. 'I have men dying every single time we go into a conflict. You're supposed to fix that. You're supposed to end that. And you type numbers into a fucking computer and hope for the best. Do better.'

'We'll fix the age issue. We're close.'

'I've heard that before. Your predecessor was always close. And now he's dead.'

Harry rushed forward to stand between them. 'Why are the military involved in… in this?' he said.

Grant looked at Harry. 'Imagine a field of battle, Harry. Have you ever walked through an infirmary tent? I've walked through and seen three hundred soldiers on their backs. Some are blinded by shrapnel. Some have lost an arm, a leg, or both. Some are dying, while the quality of life of others is so low, it borders on pathetic.' He walked across the room and tapped the glass of a tank. Bubbles formed around the disturbance, and bounced around the face of a child.

'But imagine a clone, not a useless fucking kid like this one, but a full-grown man. An exact replica of the trained soldier. There he is, bleeding out and dying in a bed. Then we flick a switch, and he spills out of a tank like this. Ready to carry on the fight. Imagine that. It's game-changing.'

'It's not right,' said Harry.

'It's life-altering,' said Evelyn. 'Think of a future, where a person is old, but they don't want their life to end. They can choose the age of their restart and do it all again.'

'But then nothing matters,' said Harry. 'How does your life matter when you can always press restart? When you can never die?'

'The priest is dead,' said Grant. 'You can still die. This is more about planning and choice. It's about winning. No matter the cost.'

'It's about life,' said Evelyn. 'Look around, Dad. This is where it begins.'

Harry looked around at the tanks. His eyes roamed the long line of faces. Until he stopped. He looked at the face of a ten-year-old boy, and saw his own reflected back at him in the glass. He turned around to face Evelyn. 'What the fuck is this? That's me. Why?'

'It's all part of the research,' she said.

'Why the fuck am I here?'

'Because everyone who works here has volunteered.

The nature of our research… it can be easier to understand results with… Well, with family. Look at the tank next to yours, Dad,' said Evelyn.

Harry looked back at his tank, and then at the one beside it, it was empty. He was confused, but in his confusion, he looked left at the next tank. Again, he had to wipe his breath from the glass, but when he did he felt his stomach drop. It was a younger Evelyn, sleeping peacefully.

'We've had so many breakthroughs,' said Evelyn, the excitement evident in her voice. 'If we can just crack the age problem, and then it's just…' She was cut off.

'Then the other giant problem,' said Grant.

'What problem?' said Harry, his eyes still glued to the young, ghostly face of his daughter.

'You saw it firsthand before,' said Grant. 'Their memories are fucked. The priest, he didn't know where he was. He didn't know a damn thing. What good is a soldier clone if it can't remember how to hold a gun?'

'Memories have been a hurdle,' said Evelyn. 'We've only managed to grow the clones as ten-year-olds, for the moment. A by-product is that they only possess memories from their life up until that point. It's a challenge.'

'One you've beaten before,' said Grant. 'I don't know why you can't replicate the same results.'

'We've tried, it didn't work. And it's been difficult to study, and you know why.'

'Evelyn?' said Harry, distracted and completely removed from their conversation. 'What was in this one?' He pointed at the emptied tank that lay beside the one that held his clone.

Grant smirked. 'That? That housed the only successful

experiment we've had yet.' The elevator doors slid open behind them. A soldier walked forward into the room. In front of him, he prodded a prisoner forward. It was the girl. Grant pointed to her.

'Harry, I think you've met Catherine? Our only real breakthrough.'

Harry's eyes moved from the empty tank to the girl, and then to his daughter. 'What did you do?'

'I flicked a switch, Dad.'

'You can leave us,' Grant said to the soldier, and he promptly headed back to the elevator.

As the elevator doors closed, the soldier could be heard muttering. The door closed in his face as he shivered in the cold and finished '… they cannot be.'

The girl hovered on the edges of the group, looking small.

'Finally, we had a breakthrough,' said Grant. 'We had a subject who could remember everything. A giant step forward. But then… this lunatic had to blind her and practically mute her. She was little more than a broken toy, so we stared down the line, hoping to strike gold again.'

Harry looked at the girl sadly, as she stared into darkness. He began to step towards her, but Grant pulled his gun and aimed for his head.

'Plant your feet, Harry. She may be broken, but she still has value to us. You though… It would be foolish to squander another chance to see the immediate effects.'

'Your man, just now… he was saying those words. The same words as the priest. And I heard it earlier, from another of your men,' said Harry.

'We developed it, as a coping mechanism for the men. For

everyone who worked here. For everyone who encountered these… children,' said Grant. 'They had to remember that they were dealing with rats in a maze. Not real life. They do not fear, they cannot hear. They do not feel, they are not real. They cannot see, they should not be. The priest heard it and in his own twisted way, it became something else. Something between him and his god.' Grant looked down on the priest's body for a moment, before cocking his gun and aiming it at Evelyn. 'Start the machine.'

'What?' she said.

'Get it started. I want to see if he loses it like the priest,' he said, nodding to Harry.

Evelyn shook her head. 'I won't do it,' she said.

'For all we know, it's genetic. Your mother was the first success. He might be the second. Do it.'

'That's not how genetics work,' she said.

Grant stepped in towards her, and held the gun to her head. He brushed her skin with it.

'You won't shoot me,' she said.

Grant smiled. 'Want to find out?'

'I do,' she said, trying to smile back. 'I'm the only scientist here, the only one in the goddamn world, who has any idea how to get what you want. If you want to set yourself back years, then pull the trigger. It'd be like burning this facility to the ground.'

Grant chewed his lip for a moment, then slammed his hand into her throat and grasped it.

'Get the fuck off her,' said Harry, stepping forward, but Grant silenced him by aiming the gun at his head.

'Not another step, Harry. I'll kill your whole family in three seconds if you try anything. Now, tell your daughter to see some fucking sense. She can live, and maybe you can too. But she needs to flick the switch.' He turned back to face Evelyn. 'The work continues, Doctor.'

'Just do it, Evelyn,' pleaded Harry.

'Yeah, Evelyn, just do it,' said Grant.

He stopped grinning when the bullet ripped through his throat. The second and third sprayed shots missed him. His hand loosened and both he and Evelyn crashed to the floor. Behind them, holding a gun that she had fired blind, was the girl. She dropped the gun, and walked forwards with her arms outstretched.

Harry moved forward and took her hand, guiding her to Evelyn, who removed herself from the tangle of Grant as he wheezed and leaked blood. But he was soon silent.

Once Evelyn had caught her breath, she looked at Harry. 'I couldn't do it,' she said. 'I couldn't watch you die.' She smiled at him sadly.

'Like I watched your mother die?' he said. 'How could you do that?'

Evelyn's smile vanished. 'You told me she felt no pain. To take comfort in that. But that was a lie, wasn't it?'

Harry looked at her. 'Yes,' he said. He looked down at the girl, still wrapping his head around the knowledge that she was a clone of his wife. 'She felt everything. Like her body was being twisted inside out, for no reason. But you're the reason. She'd have ripped her skin to the bone if I hadn't held her hands. Have you ever done that, Evelyn? Have you ever held someone tight to stop them from trying to rip themselves apart?'

'Yes,' she said, her voice low. 'The man you saw when you

arrived. With the claw marks in his chest.' She stopped, and looked away.

'He was your friend?' said Harry. Evelyn didn't answer.

'More,' croaked the girl.

'He wasn't thinking straight,' said Evelyn. 'He was tired… scared. He wanted a way out. He tried to perform the procedure on himself. We found him halfway through and tried to stop it, but… he tried again, and failed.'

'He was right to try himself,' said Harry. 'If this is what you all want, then better to do it to yourselves than to innocents like your mother.'

'That was the plan. Plans change,' she said.

'Why?' asked Harry.

'Because of my predecessor. He tried it. It failed. We all stood here helpless while he died. After that, we were directionless. But then, a breakthrough. We had to keep testing, had to keep collecting data. We made a choice. The most practical way to test the memories of the subjects, was if we knew the subjects. We made a sacrifice. The work had to continue.'

'So, when it came down to the choice between your family and a science project, you chose the science project. That's what it boils down to.'

Catherine reached out a hand and tried to take Harry's.

He looked down at her, with her blinded eyes and slit throat. 'And you're just okay with this? You're not furious?'

'Won't change anything,' she struggled to say.

Harry let out a frustrated sigh and turned away. After a moment, he turned back to the clone of his wife. 'Why didn't you tell me who you really were? All those times I was in your room,' he said.

She shook her head. 'Barely speak. Didn't think… you would believe.'

Harry opened his mouth to retort, but had none.

Evelyn stepped between them. 'You both made me everything I am,' she said.

'No, we didn't. We taught you kindness and love, not this,' said Harry, struggling to control himself.

'You made me what I am to a point, and then I had to do the rest,' she continued. 'It's hard for you to understand, but I believe in what I do. I believe in science. I saw an opening for something that I desperately wanted to do, that I desperately wanted to be a part of. A part of history, Dad, surely you can understand that.'

'No, I can't,' he said. 'History is something you look back on and study. It's not a thing you try to manipulate and place yourself in the centre of.'

'I won't apologise for refusing to be weighed down. Do you know what this place would be without me?'

'Safer?' said Harry.

'A relic. Forgotten in time,' she fired back. 'I think the mistake you make, is that you think when people start out in the same place, that they'll grow and remain the same. I never wanted that.'

'I remember when you used to win the science fair in school. Every year. I'd tell the other parents that you were going to change the world. And maybe you still will. But you're going to make it worse,' said Harry.

Evelyn stared straight at him. The venom of his words seeped through her. 'And what have you done for the world?' she said. 'When I look at you both, all I ever see is regret. I saw two people who had given up every dream they ever had because they fell in love, for a time, and got married and had a child, and then sacrificed further for that child — me — and never got close to getting what they wanted from life.'

'I did,' said Catherine. She reached out a hand, but Evelyn pushed it away.

'I've been the noose around your necks since I came into the world,' said Evelyn. 'I've learned many things from you, but the most important thing I ever learned was to not deviate from what I want. Family, life, love... nobody will get in between me and history. How many breakthroughs, how many scientific wonders have been derailed by the chemical reactions in people? People are weak. But science is strong. It will withstand the test of time. I will withstand the test of time. You taught me sacrifice. Yours was creating me. And mine is using you to build something stronger.'

'Blood,' said Harry.

'What?' said Evelyn.

'Blood,' he repeated. The hard edge had left his voice, replaced by fear. 'You're bleeding.'

Evelyn looked down at her waist. Blood stained her shirt. She touched the wound, and winced in pain. The bullet had ripped through her side. 'I was shot. I... I didn't feel it. How did I not...?' She swayed on the spot for a moment, before falling.

Harry dived forward and caught her. 'You must have been hit before,' he said. He looked at her back, where more blood drenched her shirt. The bullet had gone through. He peeled her jacket away and applied pressure to the wound.

Catherine hovered anxiously. 'My fault... stupid,' she whispered, as Evelyn began coughing up blood. The first wave sprayed out like a fountain, pushed back by the pressure.

Harry wiped it from her mouth. 'You're going to be okay,' he said.

'Dad…' she said.

He wiped away more blood. 'It's going to be fine.'

'Dad,' she said again.

'You're going to be okay.'

'Dad… I'm going to die.' She smiled bitterly, and her teeth were stained red.

Harry's grip tightened. 'I won't let you. I'm still angry at you, Eve. You can't go anywhere.' His hands shook as he and Catherine tried desperately to keep the blood at bay.

'There's only one way,' said Evelyn. 'You have to flick the switch, Dad.' She pointed to the computer, and then to the younger form of her that floated in the tank.

Harry shook his head. 'No. I won't,' he said.

'You have to. It's the only way. Or this is all for nothing. All the pain.'

'What if it doesn't work? What if you don't remember?' said Harry, his voice quaking.

Evelyn coughed again, as blood filled her mouth. 'Please,' she managed to say.

Harry felt a tight hand close around his. Catherine put her head against his. 'Please, Harry,' she said.

He looked from her to their daughter, and nodded. He stood and hurried to the computer. His hands shook violently. He looked at the screen, but all he saw was scientific gibberish.

'Find my name,' said Evelyn, 'and hit the button.'

Harry scrolled through dozens of names before hers

stood out. He selected it. His finger hovered over the button. He looked down at Evelyn, his baby, perhaps for the final time. He pushed the button, and for a moment, nothing happened. Then she screamed and writhed and twisted violently. Her mother tried valiantly to pin her arms, but was losing the battle. Harry rushed over to help. Together, the parents held their daughter's arms while she felt pain the likes of which no one should ever endure. They clung on desperately to stop her from tearing herself apart. And they held on even when the life seeped out of her and she lay limp in a pool of blood.

They looked up and watched the tank as bubbles formed. They momentarily lost sight of her body. The glass lifted and thick green liquid spilled out, the naked child with it. She climbed from the ground, and blinked as if using her eyes for the first time. They both held their breath as they waited for her to move, to speak, to give some sign that she remembered.

Evelyn looked around the room, from the computer to the row of tanks and strings of cables. She looked at her older body, dead on the ground in the hands of her parents. 'Mum? Dad? Who's that?'

'Doesn't know,' said Catherine. She smiled.

'It didn't work… why are you smiling?' said Harry.

She grinned wider. 'Because… it didn't work,' she said.

Harry looked at his daughter, and understanding hit him. She didn't remember any of it. The pain. The violence. The deaths. Nor her role in it. It was a second chance. 'Come here, Eve,' he said, and she rushed into his arms.

She cuddled his chest for warmth, and stared up at him

with an inquisitive look, her brow furrowed. 'Is the swing finished yet, Daddy?' she said.

The words rolled over Harry like a wave, and moved him more than anything ever had. He held her out at arm's length and her face made him grin.

But the grin was lost as the gunshot echoed off the walls, and Evelyn's body twisted as the bullets crashed into her.

It happened so fast that Harry's hand still held hers tight as the force of the impact spun her around, before she crumpled into his arms. He opened his mouth to tell her it would all be okay, but half her head was gone.

'Meat for crows,' slurred Grant, swaying on his feet and holding his gun. The bullet hole in his throat was open wide, and blood covered most of his body. His eyes rolled around and with every cough, a little more blood came out of him.

'Meat for crows,' he started to say again, but only got halfway through before Harry had charged across the room and tackled him to the ground.

Harry balled his fists and punched him with every ounce of strength and energy he could muster. There were no words for the man who had killed his daughter. No words would bring justice. There was only pain.

Grant's limp arm pointed to the tanks, and he tried to form words that sounded like 'find my tank, find my tank.' But Harry didn't care, and he kept on punching him. Harry punched him until every bone in his hand was broken, and until Grant's face looked like red slush.

When he stopped punching, he just breathed and looked above to the dark ceiling. He looked through the ceiling, through the clouds. He looked high above, and he knew in his heart that there was nothing there.

Once the adrenalin had started to fade, Harry felt something in his stomach. He looked down, and only then noticed that Grant had plunged a blade into it. He hadn't seen it. Hadn't felt it. But now it was all he felt. The pain coursed through him, and he struggled to stand. But he did, and he staggered back to his wife and daughter. He fell to his knees, and held both their hands. One living, and one colder by the second.

Harry looked down at what was left of his young daughter's beautiful face, he closed her one remaining eye, and then he cried.

His wife held him tight. Her hand searched for his, but found the knife handle instead.

'It's okay,' he said, trying to be strong like Evelyn. 'I'm going to die.'

'No,' she said, as loud as she could. She pointed to the machine. 'Live.'

Harry shook his head and squeezed her hand, as blood started to leak from the wound. 'I've accepted it,' he said.

She squeezed his hand back. 'I haven't. Don't leave me.'

Harry smiled at her. 'What if I don't remember?'

'You'll live.'

He nodded. 'We have to destroy this place. We have to burn it.' She nodded in agreement.

Harry crawled to the computer. He scrolled through names, and hovered over his own. He looked back at her. 'I hope I remember you.'

'You will.'

Harry pushed the button. He wrenched the knife free from the wound, and blood poured out.

Catherine took a firm hold of his arms, as he began to scream. When he was done, the glass of his tank lifted and his young body fell forward, head slamming into the floor. She heard the sound, and scrambled to his side. 'Harry?' she asked. But he didn't respond, he just lay on the cold floor. 'Harry?' she said, louder. He said nothing. She held her ear to his chest, and strained to hear a heartbeat.

He was alive. His eyes opened a sliver, but his vision was blurred. He felt himself fall in and out of the edges of consciousness.

Catherine scrambled to her feet. Her hands reached for anything firm. 'We have to destroy this place, destroy it and find the elevator.' She turned at the sound of movement.

'Elevator is that way,' said Harry, as he hauled himself upright, and pointed towards the hallway.

'Harry,' she said, walking towards the sound of his voice with a smile. 'Harry, do you remember? Do you remember me?' She ran a hand along his face, tracing his young features. When he didn't respond her hand slipped and her smile wavered. 'Harry... Do you remember what Evelyn would ask you, when she was young?'

'Is the swing finished yet, Daddy?' he said, and although Catherine couldn't see the bittersweet smile on his face, it perfecty matched her own.

The Pyramid

Printed in Great Britain
by Amazon